THE RETURN

SANSHLIAN SERIES: BOOK 3

FoxTales Press

DANI HOOTS

The Return
Sanshlian Series, #3
First Publication © 2020 FoxTales Press
Content and line edits by Justin Boyer
Cover Design Copyright © 2020 by Biserka Designs

ISBN for paperback: 978-1-942023-65-4

To my High School BFF Corinne,

Ha! Told ya I could finish what I started! Eventually…

Chapter 1

Three years earlier.

These guys were amateurs.

I glanced back in my rearview mirror to see the next contestant barely making it around the corner a couple hundred meters behind me. I licked my lips and smiled. This was way too easy—I could get used to a life like this.

The sad part for these guys, I had just learned to drive. I was new to this, and I was still beating them. No wonder the Emperor thought it would be a good idea for me to enter this contest—he had faith I would figure it out.

Taking a deep breath, I tried not to think of what this was really about. I couldn't let my current victory cloud my judgment, as there was a lot at stake here. Although, if I still got second or third in this last race, I would still get first place overall, as my points were exceeding everyone else. But I knew if I let them get near me, someone would try to sabotage my car. I was too good for them, which caused them to resort to illegal tactics.

But that was Recar for you. Legal means accomplished nothing here.

Which was where I came in.

This was my first mission on my own that the Emperor had assigned me. After years of training, I was ready, although I felt I had been ready for awhile now. The mission was to get close to the leader of Recar, Jack McHannon, and assassinate him, as he was causing some trouble for the Pandronan Empire. It was about time the Empire dealt with this planet, and I would be key in that victory. I couldn't wait.

The reason I had to compete in this race, however, was because there was no good way to get close to Jack. He was heavily guarded. However, if I won this race I could become his personal driver. Then I could kill him.

Easy as that.

The Emperor had trained me to stay incognito, but this mission was proving to make that a strenuous task. I was the youngest person to compete, and it was technically against the rules. However, rules didn't matter here, but it was gaining a lot of press and although I tried my best to stay away from cameras by keeping my helmet on as much as possible, those sneaky journalists followed me everywhere and snapped a few pictures. Now everyone knew what I looked like.

I guess I would just be that face everyone feared.

No one knew who I was, but that would change soon. I was the Emperor's Shadow—the person that would be getting the dirty things done. I was to crush any resistance throughout the galaxy. It was what the Emperor trained me to do.

And I didn't have a choice.

I would have been dead if the Emperor didn't find me and adopt me, so to speak. I had tried to kill him a few times, yet he still took me under his wing. Why that was, I did not understand. I tried to bring it up multiple times, but he always ignored the question. I gave up asking him and just accepted my fate—I was his tool.

"Bitch, you better not win this! You aren't even old enough to race! I'm going to—"

I clicked off the radio. Great, they tapped into my car komlink that was only supposed to be used by me and the race coordinators in case there were any hazards or reasons to stop the race. If the man was smart, he would have pretended he was one of the coordinators and created a fake hazard so I would slow down and he could pass me. But instead, as all men like to do, he just threatened me.

I swerved a little right, barely clearing the corner. I needed to keep my mind focused on the race and stop thinking about how stupid people were, and about my past. It was what moved me forward, however, as I had learned to look out for myself and myself only. I didn't trust anyone—I didn't need to. All I needed was myself and I would do anything to keep it that way. I hated working with the Emperor's other generals, as they all wanted to see me fall. They seemed to be jealous of the way the Emperor treated me, although I wasn't sure why. His attention didn't mean I was living a splendid life, it just meant I had more at stake.

Which was why I couldn't mess this up.

Taking a deep breath, I glanced in my rearview mirror again to find one car starting to decrease the distance between us. He must have been using illegal boosters, which were fair game on this planet. It just meant he would lose even harder. I pushed the gas a little more, as he wasn't the only one with a spruced-up engine. The Emperor gave me all the finances I needed to win. I laughed as the car took off.

I still didn't quite understand what the point of these races were. It seemed excessive to have the entire capital Himeo shut down for a week so they could race through the streets. It was all for the leader to decide who would be his next driver. Although the planet was under his rule, there were other bosses in different cities who tried to murder him often. So they needed someone reliable driving him around.

Yeah, this planet was crazy and needed to be ruled under the Empire.

I glanced up at the capitol building to see a figure in the upper window. It was probably Jack McHannon himself watching us race. There was no way to tell, as he was too far up and I had to keep my eyes on the road, but it was a feeling in my gut.

In the past couple of years, I noticed my gut feelings getting stronger and stronger, which has saved my life more than once. I just hoped I wouldn't lose faith in it, or trust it too much, and then be led astray. Intuition could only get me so far in this line of work, yet it was very beneficial. The Emperor said to always trust my feelings when I didn't know what to do next. At first, I didn't understand what he meant, but as time went on, I understood my gut feelings were always right.

The Emperor had taught me everything I knew. Although I had many trainers, it was he who taught me the nitty-gritty, and how to decide to kill someone or to take them in for questioning. Never did I think that would be something I would have to learn after growing up on Garvner. Now it was all I had to think about. What would my father think of this version of me?

I shook my head. Right now was not the time to think about my father. I had to get him out of my head if I wanted to keep going. I knew in my heart he was watching over me, disappointed in the person I had become. But it wasn't my fault—it was just how the cards fell.

I trained for weeks for this mission—months of almost killing myself in high-speed crashes. I didn't know how to drive before Emperor Neil put me behind the wheel and let me go. All I had ever driven were motorbikes, which I pleaded to race with instead of these stupid cars. They were too clunky and didn't have the same maneuverability. Every time I asked, however, I got slapped. Neil said the races were done with cars because it was all about keeping the leader safe. If he was on a motorbike, he would be a vulnerable target. I disagreed, as there were bulletproof vests and such, but I guess he had a point. I just didn't want to admit it, especially not to him.

Only a few hundred meters to the finish mark. I had this—there was no way I would make any mistakes that would lose me this race.

As if on cue, I heard gunshots fire and hit the back of my car. The second round caused the glass to shatter.

"Sons of bitches!" I yelled back at them, even though I knew they couldn't hear me. I did not have time for this.

I knew I should just ignore it and get to the end of the race, but this was just pissing me off. I pulled out my gun, a TG-2, and pointed it at the bastard who was shooting at me. If he thought he would get away with this, he had another thing coming.

Also, this would show I could fight and race simultaneously. Not that it mattered; I would get the contract, anyway.

I fired three shots straight at where the guy's head stuck out his window. I saw his head jerk back then slump over as his car went out of control and into the barriers. I tried not to think about the people who were standing there watching. Although the streets were supposed to be cleared for this event, some people thought it was a superb idea to stand right behind the barriers and watch, especially near the finish mark. An explosion caused a fiery ball to radiate onto the racetrack and many of the cars either swerved into the other barriers or slammed on their brakes. It didn't matter to me though—I had crossed the finish line.

I had won all the races.

My car came to a stop, and I got out before the reporters could corner me. I ran towards the barrier they weren't allowed to cross, keeping my helmet on. I didn't want more photos of me, especially with what had just happened. My heart was beating fast now, and I could hardly breathe.

Although I had killed quite a few people in past missions, this felt strange. They were just bystanders. Everything felt dizzy. Maybe I wasn't cut out for this. I took a couple of deep breaths and ran towards the bathroom I knew was on the other side of the stage.

Lifting the toilet seat, I threw up.

I heard a knock on the door. "Everything all right, love?"

It was a man's voice. It sounded familiar, but with the heavy accent many of these Recarian's had, sometimes I just mistook them for another person.

I flushed the toilet. "I'm fine, just got a little car sick."

"It's your first race, right? I don't blame you for getting sick. So many emotions were going through your head, especially when you killed that guy."

I rolled my eyes. Great, that was all that anyone would talk about. I sighed as I rinsed my hands off and opened the door to deal with this guy, who I figured was a reporter.

It wasn't easy to surprise me, but the person waiting outside the door, smiling at me, made my mouth drop. It was Jack McHannon, the ruler of this planet. He had a gentle smile on his scruffy face. He didn't appear to be too much older than me, and it was a wonder how he got to be in his position at such a young age.

"Mister McHannon, I'm sorry, I didn't realize—" I fumbled with my words as too many thoughts were going through my head.

"No apology necessary. I just wanted to make sure my star racer was doing all right. That ending was quite a show, even by my standards. I hope you join my organization after the ceremony. You do have a choice, you know."

I glanced around. We were alone. No one would notice if I killed him right now. I still had my gun on me. It would be easy.

"Yeah, I will join your group. That was the whole reason I entered."

He brushed a piece of my hair back. "That's splendid news. I'm looking forward to spending more time with each other."

I tried not to barf again. Did he think lines like that worked? Although, he wasn't too bad to look at. He had a cocky grin on his face that made a lot of girls smile. I just was not one of them and never would be.

Jack handed me a couple of mints. "Here, for the taste you have in your mouth."

I took them. "Thank you."

"Don't mention it. Now, everyone is waiting for you. Also, keep the helmet off. You have such a gorgeous face."

Maybe I should kill him now. I was getting a little tired of his flirtatious comments. "You are too kind. I'd just rather not deal with the comments some men give me and be recognized for my work, not my face."

"Well, when you work under me, you won't have to worry about comments from people. They won't mess with you once you are connected to me."

I found that hard to believe. "You must have a lot of power over your people then."

"That I do. You will come to find that out soon enough." He held out his hand. "Now, let us not keep them waiting any longer."

As I took his hand, my left hand reached for my TG-2. I could kill him right here and now. Just as I was going to make my decision, a person came around the corner.

Taking my hand off my holster, I smiled.

"I'm looking forward to working with you, Mister McHannon."

Chapter 2

Present

I took my first step on Recar and took a deep breath. Yup, it still smelled of dense city filth and motor oil. It was great to be back here, even if it wasn't the Recar I knew. Although, nothing about this planet really changed. It would always be the same, no matter what century it was. There would always be tall buildings, chaos in the streets, races, and some cocky bastard ruling. It was lucky for me, though, as that meant I could sweet talk myself out of anything here, and I knew how to play the system. I doubted I would have any trouble winning this race.

The trouble would be getting the right amount of points to get second place.

The entire tournament took tally of all four races, added them up, and then the winner was determined. There were a lot of variables that could come up for trying to determine who was second, third, etc. Should I win two races and then get third twice? Would that be the right amount of points? What if the person who won first didn't get enough to outdo me and ended up having someone else first, pushing me to third? It was a giant math equation that was ever changing.

"What is it, daughter?" Nygard asked me as he grabbed his bags. It was strange now knowing he was my father as only a few months earlier he was just some trainer named Dan to me. Since then, he had trained me in using my powers and I felt stronger than I even thought was possible. I still didn't know if I considered him as evil as the stories made him out to be, but at some moments I could see the darkness in his eyes and it made me shudder.

We were heading to the room Tim and Logan had set up. Tim Nevo, who was once Thomas Draff, and Logan Pale, who was once Peter Hass, were also sent to the past with me along with General Laura Curtis, who was now Jane Doresmith, and Emperor Neil Valym, who now was Emperor Joss Valym, along with my brothers crew and Jack. All the names were still confusing, but since we all had different bodies, it made it a little easier to associate the new names with people. I just had to remember who was actually inhabiting the body.

Nygard sent Tim and Logan ahead of us to Recar, in an effort not to raise suspicion of a bunch of Imperials coming to the planet, even if we were using fake names. Tim and Logan were also racing and if we all arrived together, it would look like we were trying something dirty as not many outsiders came to compete in the races.

I mean, we were. But we didn't want them to know that.

"Nothing. It's just that this was Jack's home, and I spent a lot of time here. It's the closest thing I have to a home."

He nodded. "I understand the feeling of always being on the run and not having a place to settle down. Soon we will call this entire galaxy our home, when it is under our rule."

I said nothing, as I wasn't sure what else to say. I glanced over to find Joss watching us. I almost forgot he was there. Seeing him brought back memories of the past when he was once Emperor Neil, the one I used to serve. I was his Shadow—his assassin. I had always thought he had saved me, because he saw something great in me, only to find out he had been using me the entire time. He knew I was the daughter of Nygard and the only one who could find Sanshli and be able to open the temple door. Then he just left me there to go insane and wither away.

The joke was on him, though, as Nygard was reanimated and cared about his one and only daughter.

However, if I regained consciousness a little earlier, I would have been able to stop my brother from taking the sword out of the statue and not be stuck in this weird alternate past. Then I could have fulfilled my destiny in bringing order to the galaxy, whatever that meant. Supposedly I was the only one who could destroy Nygard, and that was what my mother wanted me to do.

Except now that I had spent time with Nygard, I didn't find him to be half the evil entity that all the stories made him out to be.

He explained it to me many times how his people had turned on him and he had to do what he did to make this place safe for generations to come—safe for me. I didn't quite understand his reasoning since he murdered all of his people, so there were no generations to come. Only a few Sanshlians remain scattered throughout the galaxy, most of whom feared Nygard. Mother had told me about how he twists lies to make him seem like the hero, and not to trust anything he says, but I haven't seen her in months. I had no idea why she left, and I wondered deep down if it was because of something Nygard did. Maybe he somehow knew she was talking to me and made her disappear. There were a lot of unanswered questions in my life—a lot more than I could have ever imagined.

We grabbed the rest of our bags and headed towards the hotel. I just hoped it would be rather large with all of us being in there. One could only handle so much time with these people, and I hated being in confined quarters with Tim. He had nothing good to say, as he was jealous of me. He kept trying to beat me in sparring even though I have won again and again. He blamed it on my powers, even though I rarely had to use them.

And beating him during our race practices was just the

icing on the cake.

Hailing a cab, I got in next to Nygard while Joss got up front with the driver. I watched as rain hit the windows. It didn't feel like Recar without it raining. It rained more days of the year here than Anosira had sun, which was most days. It was also why I felt people were so ruthless here, as they didn't have the sun to make them smile. When it was sunny out, though, everyone was in a joyful mood and I swore there was a lot less crime.

"Such a gloomy place, are you sure you feel as if this is your home?" Nygard asked as he saw me looking out the window. I took a deep breath and turned to him.

"It's more the company than the place, I suppose."

I heard Joss try to hide a snicker, but I glared at him. He had been reading my mind ever since we first met, so he knew my true feelings for Jack. He knew about the adventures we had together, and how much we cared for one another. He thought it was funny that I could care for someone like Jack. He didn't understand Jack was the only person who had cared for me, no matter what my past was. We didn't judge each other for the lives we lived, but accepted each other for what we were. No one could take that away.

Father didn't make any other comments for the rest of the ride. It was about ten minutes before the taxi had stopped and we were in front of a standard-looking hotel. It didn't stand out, which was good since we wanted to blend in. There were hundreds of hotels in this city alone, ranging from 'I think if I slept in that bed, I might contract a disease' to 'I swear I just saw god walking down the hall'.

This was the hotel of commoners, which was the way we wanted it to be.

I grabbed my luggage from the trunk. The driver tried to help, but I didn't like other people touching my stuff. I also didn't trust anyone on Recar, as most liked to pickpocket and steal, cab drivers included.

Tim and Logan were able to secure a few rooms with joining doors. I had my own room, thank the stars. I did not want to deal with sharing a room with anyone, not even Nygard. Although, I knew being with them would make it so I wouldn't be able to meet up with Jack that easily, and I had a feeling my every move would be watched by one of these guys.

Some things never changed.

No one here other than my father trusted me. I didn't blame them, they had a lot of reasons to not trust me anymore, but I also had a lot of reasons not to trust them or side with them. It had become a mutual distress.

I set my things on my bed and sighed. Now we would have to go down to check our cars. Tim and Logan were to get the mechanical things ready, but I wanted to check mine out for myself. I had a feeling they would try to sabotage it otherwise. Especially Tim.

Tim stepped into my room, and I threw him a look. He just laughed and threw me an orange. "Figured you would be hungry after the long trip."

It was probably poison. I threw it back at him. "No thanks, I'm fine."

"Suit yourself. I was just making a peace offering, as

the last time we were on this planet, I was chasing you."

"You trying to bring up the one time you have won in a match? Or are you just trying to get on my nerves?"

"Both. I think we will have a splendid time here."

"I swear to god, Tim, I will end you if you come anywhere near me."

He held up his hands. "Sorry, I was just trying one of the lines Jack would use in this situation. You always seem to fall for it if he says it."

I grabbed the heaviest small object near me, which was a komlink system, and threw it at his face. To my surprise, he wasn't able to dodge it and hit him straight in the face.

Served him right.

"Knock it off, you two." Jane entered the room. She always seemed to have a resting bitch face no matter where she went. There was a reason I still called her the "Ice Queen." I rolled my eyes. I always got blamed for shit that Tim did, no matter if it was me who started it or not.

"Whatever, how about both of you just get out of my room?"

To my surprise, both of them listened and let me get on with putting away my stuff. I didn't have much, just some clothes, guns I could smuggle in, and a toothbrush.

"Have everything you need?"

I looked up to find Nygard standing in the doorway. Had anyone ever heard of knocking?

"Yeah, I have everything I need. I just wanted to put it all away real quick."

"Well, when you are done, let me know. We were about to check the cars and then grab dinner."

I nodded. "That sounds good."

He left me to finish up, and I did just that. It always felt weird to unpack stuff that was mine, but yet not mine at the same time. They were just standard clothes issued to me—the way I've always gotten my clothes. I have never gone out shopping for clothes like many other girls did. Jack had tried many, many times to get me to go shopping. He offered to pay for anything I wanted, but I never cared about clothes. I didn't care about style or to stand out. I just liked my comfortable stuff that I could move easily in.

I went back to the main area and followed all of them out of the room. We went down the elevator and hailed a couple of taxis to take us to the garage that the cars were at.

It was still raining.

The sun was setting, and the streets seemed to feel more dangerous and more populated. I wondered how many of these people were night owls, since it wasn't like the sun would come out behind the clouds during the day. There was more action at night as there were many bars and events going on. And it was easier to hide in the shadows at night.

My taxi had Nygard in the back with me and Logan up front. I was glad it was with Logan as he and I rarely exchanged words. We just sort of ignored each other and called it good. It wasn't like we needed to interact, and if we did, we kept it professional. The only time he annoyed me was when Tim was involved and he blamed me for the shit Tim started. They all did, except Nygard. Tim, however, didn't start anything when Nygard was around, which made sense. He was the most powerful being in all the galaxy. He wasn't someone you wanted to piss off.

The garage was only about five minutes away, which wasn't bad in this kind of traffic. We could have walked, but I had a feeling that none of the guys here wanted to walk in the rain after setting up base on Anosira. It was always sunny there. Although I didn't like the rain, I preferred Recar as it had my type of people.

People that wanted to survive.

We arrived to the garage, and Tim unlocked the doors. Two beautiful silver cars awaited us. I furrowed my eyebrows. We were one car short. I turned to Nygard.

"I don't understand, I thought three of us were going to race. Why are we short a car?"

He laughed as he went over to the corner and pulled up a thick sheet. There stood a motorcycle.

I gasped. He did it. He got me a motorcycle instead of a car. I always wanted to race in a motorcycle and show these people it was more practical when getting away from someone. When it came to not getting shot, one had to just wear a bullet-proof vest and a bullet-proof helmet, which they had here. It made getting through traffic a heck of a lot easier, and you could squeeze through alleyways. It was much more efficient.

"I was able to get the coordinators to let you race with the motorcycle. You will have to watch out for the other cars, however, as they will try to run you over."

I shook my head. "They won't be able to even catch up to me, so that won't be a worry. This is the best surprise, thank you father." I said the last word with a little unease. It was still strange calling him my father when I was raised by a man on Garvner all those years ago. I grew up believing he was my real dad until eventually finding out I was the daughter from the legends he told me at bedtime. He wasn't supposed to die, that wasn't part of the plan, so him giving me an explanation never happened.

I wished I could talk to him one last time so I would know the truth.

"I just wanted you to be able to show them how it's done. And I wanted to see you smile. You don't seem to do it often unless Jack is around."

I didn't respond, but stroked the handles of my new beautiful bike. It was a metallic black with metallic wheels that I knew would glide the ground with such ease. I was so looking forward to this. I turned her on and she purred so gently and lit up with a nice teal blue.

This was the perfect gift. Not even Jack could outdo Nygard. Then again, Nygard could read my mind and know what I really wanted at all times, which made figuring out what I wanted to do when all this was over all that much harder.

And the fact I have hid from all of them that the map was in the second-place trophy, not the first.

So far, he hadn't let on that he knew I was lying, which showed me that I was better at lying than I had originally thought. If I could even lie to the most powerful being, and to a couple of other people who could read minds, maybe I was even more powerful than my father.

Yeah, that wasn't true.

"Do you want to go take it out for a test drive?" he asked.

I smiled. "I would love that."

"Then go ahead and meet us back at the hotel later."

I didn't wait for the others to protest as I quickly put on my helmet and rode out of there as fast as I could, my blonde hair dancing in the wind.

Chapter 3

It had been a long time since I had felt this free.

I raced down the streets of Himeo, getting yelled at by pedestrians and drivers alike. I may or may not have given a few people a scare by how close I was riding next to them, but I didn't care. I wouldn't hit them; I knew what I was doing.

I had a lot of training on a motorbike, as I used one to get around on a lot of missions. It was a wonderful way to travel, especially when it was just me. Even with one other person, it was easy to maneuver. I loved it.

I was away from the other and had no one watching me or glaring at me or trying to get on my nerves. I was sick and tired of having to deal with men who were too immature to have a polite conversation. No, this was the first time I was free to do what I wanted in over a year.

Jack, have you made it to Recar yet? I sent a message to him through our mind connection. Jack McHannon, who was now Xander Vanguard, was once the leader of this planet. He told me the person he got sent back into time as was supposedly the winner of the races and would become the leader. It seemed that everyone thrown into the past become some they were somehow connected to in the future. Except for me, of course. I was just some Sanshlian anomaly. Just like my father.

I knew it would be a stupid idea to meet up with Jack in person, but I wanted to check in and make sure he was safe. I worried that my brother and the others wouldn't treat him fairly, given his connection with me. Although he wasn't with the Imperials, he was still on a hair purer than I was. He had his skeletons in his closest, as did most people.

We just landed, Cadi, how goes it on your side?

We still used our past names as we were too familiar with each other not to. We didn't really have anyone to overhear us and question why we would use different names like Joss or my brother had. *He wasn't well known on Recar and I wasn't supposed to be alive in this era.*

It was great to hear his voice, even if it wasn't audible. We had been staying in contact since he escaped Anosira to give my brother the plan on finding Sanshli. My brother would also be here, trying desperately to win the races and get that map. We all wanted to get to Sanshli to lift this curse. The outcome of lifting the curse would just depend on who got to Sanshli first. For my brother, it would mean destroying the Empire, whereas if Nygard got there first, he would make it so he had his powers reinstated and he would become immortal. What I wanted to do, I still wasn't sure. I didn't know what was the right choice. I had seen what my brother believed in, which was a lot of death for the Imperials. I had seen what the Imperials wanted, which was the death of the P.A.E., Pirates Against the Empire. I knew what my father wanted, which was complete control over everything. No matter who won, there would be death. I didn't know what was the right choice. Which one of these people walked the right path?

Fine. Nygard ordered me a motorbike instead of a car. He was able to convince them to let me enter with it and everything.

You and that damn bike. You know everyone is just going to run you off the road, right?

I snickered. *They won't be able to catch up with me, so I doubt that will be a problem.*

Well, I have nothing that interesting to report. We will be setting up base and checking out our own cars soon. The races start tomorrow, you know.

I know, but I couldn't help but take this baby out for a spin. Besides, I had to get away. I hate being around them all.

It's almost like you just aren't a people person, Cadi. What a shocker.

I rolled my eyes. As if he didn't already know that. *I wish we could meet up, but I have a feeling I am always being watched.*

Don't you always feel that way?

That I do. But you know what I mean.

I do. But I will see you at the races tomorrow. Get some sleep and don't kill Tim.

That's funny coming from you.

I'm just saying you have to leave him for me to kill.

If anyone will kill him, it will be me, Jack.

We will see about that. In the meantime, focus on the races. There is a lot at stake, more so than ever.

He didn't have to tell me twice.

I revved the engine and kept going through the city with no real destination. I just wanted to practice maneuvering, and experiment with how well I could take corners. Part of the city was closed down already for the races as they needed to prepare the tracks. I thought about sneaking in and practicing, but I also didn't want to be disqualified. It would have been fun to do, though, and see if they could catch me. It would be obvious it was me as I was the only one on a motorbike.

As I turned down an alleyway, I noticed a car hesitate and stop, realizing they couldn't follow me. Were they following me? Was it one of Nygard's men?

Who even knew me on this planet?

I hurried down the alleyway, peering each way for anyone who would appear to be following me. At first, I didn't spot anyone, but after returning to the main drag, I spotted a couple of cars trying to close-in on me.

Great, this was all I needed within the first few hours of being on Recar.

I tried to go through the reasons someone would be after me here. Did they find a list of the racers and were taking them out one by one? Did I hit my head, and we were back in the future and everything up to now was just a dream? Did I just get a little too close to a car and now that person was after me for almost scratching their precious car?

Or did they figure out Jack and I broke in to where the trophies were and messed with them?

There was no way someone saw us or got video of us doing it as we had used our powers. The only logical explanation was that they had been following me for a while. So what was it?

And did I want to let them catch me and find out?

It was always a toss-up whether surrendering or running was the best option, as I had plenty of experience with both. There was a 50/50 chance either option could end badly for me, so I would have to make a choice.

Deciding to lose them for now, I turned down another alleyway. The cars behind me stopped, as they could not follow.

So I wasn't making this up, they were after me. Great.

I raced down the alleyway, hoping that there wouldn't be any more cars waiting for me on the other street. Just as I got out of the alleyway, another car almost clipped me.

"Shit!" I pushed forward and dashed further down the street, ignoring any thought of there being a speed limit. I heard people yell at me from the streets, gestures being pointed in my direction, but I didn't care, I just had to get out of here.

I could head back to where the garage was, but I didn't

want to sabotage our mission. So, I had to lose them before I could head back.

That was easier said than done.

The biggest problem I had was the fact that there were quite a few cars in this chase. Who had enough money to hire all these cars for little ol' me?

Normally in this situation, I would abandon my bike and run inside somewhere I knew how to sneak through to get away from whoever was chasing me. But that would mean I would have to abandon my bike, which wasn't something I would do, not when Nygard had purchased it for the races. It meant something to me, strangely enough. It was the first time I had an object I didn't want to get rid of. Other than my pocket watch, of course.

One thing that surprised me was the fact that they hadn't started shooting at me. I didn't have a bullet-proof vest, so it would be easy for whoever it was to take me down. This meant only one thing.

They wanted me alive.

I took a deep breath and tried to think of what I would do next. It was a good thing that they wanted me alive, but it was a bad thing they were after me in the first place, especially since I had no idea who it was that would be after me.

Another pedestrian yelled at me, dropping his dinner as I raced past him. It wasn't my fault he wasn't paying attention to his surroundings. I made out a few cuss words before his voice was drowned out by the city. I was getting to the populated area, which I hoped would slow down the cars. Traffic was horrible in this part of the city.

Glancing back, I saw five men on motorcycles. Even the bad guys realized that motorcycles were better for getting around this city.

I rounded another corner and went into an alleyway I knew went through to another street. I hoped I did it fast enough that the other motorcycles would have to round back and I would game some time. Looking back, I found that one was still on my tail, but the others were further behind. Lucky for me.

As carefully as I could, I grabbed the dumpster that was on the side and moved it in the way behind me. For a normal human, this would not have been a simple task. But I was no mere human.

Super strength came in handy a lot more than all the other powers did.

I heard the motorcycles behind me stop short and my pursuers started screaming at me. I laughed. Now I just had to disappear before any of the cars reached me.

Just as I thought I was in the clear, a car blocked the other side of the alleyway. My bike screeched to a halt. Damn it, they had cornered me.

I guess now I would know who was chasing me, not that I would surrender without a fight of course.

The men that had been on the motorcycles were the first to reach me. I quickly got off my bike before they thought they had me at a disadvantage.

I really wished I had my gun and knife on me right now.

I didn't bring them because I figured we were just going to look at the cars, get dinner, and head back to the hotel. The odds of someone cornering me like this were near zero at the beginning of the night, not to mention I didn't think I would split up from the others.

At least I was deadly even without a weapon.

Stepping towards the closest guy, I punched him straight in the gut. I didn't use too much of my super strength, as I didn't want to punch a hole through him, but I did leave him gasping for breath.

That's when the guns and knives came out.

It would be stupid to let them shoot me, as then they would know I could heal myself. No, I would have to surrender since I didn't have any weapons.

"Hands on your head! On your knees!" One of the men ordered. All of them were still wearing their helmets, which made it hard to distinguish them. They were all muscular and almost the same height.

I did as they ordered and put my hands on my head and went down to my knees. The door to the car opened and I saw a familiar face.

"Now, now, don't treat a lady like that. She is our guest," Kane Hulligan, the leader of this planet said with a slight grin.

"But sir, she is really strong, she might try to get away."

Kane stepped up to the group. "She was only running because she didn't know what was going on. It was basic instinct."

He held out his hand to me. "I am sorry for my men's actions, Miss Ryetirf."

I used my old name from when I worked for the Empire simply because no one, other than those from the future, knew of it. It wasn't rare for those in the races to use a fake name, and at this point I felt that I didn't know what my real name was. I was born Myra, daughter of Nygard, but grew up half my life as Arcadia Archer, and was given the name Arcadia Ryetirf from the Emperor. I felt each even had a different type of personality, when one got down to it. Since this was a mission, I felt Arcadia Ryetirf was suitable.

I took his hand and got up. "You know, chasing a girl all around the city isn't the best way to get her attention. You could have just waited for when I wasn't on my bike."

"Oh, we were going to, but you noticed too early, and kept going down alleyways. It made it a little hard."

"That's fair. Now, what do you need of me, Mister Hulligan? The races start tomorrow, you could have just waited until then."

He let out a little laugh. "Straight to the point as always. I had some questions for you. The races this year, or at least some of the contestants, have caught my attention. I was wondering if you could come back with me and take a look."

Shit, he was smarter than we gave him credit for. "What do you mean?"

"It's more something I have to show you. Will you come with me?"

"Do I have a choice?"

He let out another laugh. "No, if I am honest, you do

not."

"I understand. The problem is, how am I going to get my bike back to the garage if I go with you in the car?" I doubted he would be stupid enough to let me drive myself to his office. But he knew as well as me, I needed it tomorrow.

"My men will take it back to the garage, or at least a garage. It will be there for you at the races tomorrow, all ready to go."

I made a fake smile. "You are too kind, Mister Hulligan."

He led me to his car and opened the door for me. "As long as you answer my questions, my lady, you have nothing to fear."

I slid into the car, the smell of old leather filling my lungs. "I will do my best."

He closed the door and got in on the other side. He tapped his cane on the roof of the car and we started down the street.

Chapter 4

"So how has your time on the planet been? You just arrived today, correct?" Kane asked as the car headed towards his office.

"Yes, I just arrived. So far it has been good, other than believing I was running for my life."

He laughed. "I'm sorry about that. It did get out of hand, but I wanted to talk to you as quickly as I could."

I wondered what he wanted to talk about, and if it would compromise the mission. If he suspected anything, forcing us to withdraw, it would be even harder to get the gem out of the trophy. I tried to stay calm. If I acted nervous, he would have more reason to suspect I was hiding something.

Kane reached for the small bar he had in his car. "Let me make it up to you. Whiskey, wasn't it?"

Offering alcohol, or plain flirting, I swore, was the only way these leaders thought they could make up for something. Usually it was both. I nodded as he grabbed a miniature bottle of whiskey and poured some in a glass.

"You know," he said as he handed me the glass, "I didn't think I would see you again. That is, until I saw your name pop up on the race qualifiers. I was sad that I wouldn't get to talk to you more. You left so quickly and I found no trace of you. It was rather odd."

"I'm good at getting in and out of somewhere with no one noticing. Years of training."

"Right. Tell me, though, where did you train to be a racer?"

He was asking strange questions. I wasn't uncommon for people to travel around different planets. I had a nasty feeling about all of this. "Here and there. My old job required some driving."

"Your old job? The one where you partner was murdered? Or was it a different job?" he asked. It impressed me he remembered so much about me.

"All my jobs, to be honest. But yes, the fact I could get away so fast did come in handy in that mission."

"I see. I do like that you were able to get away, but don't like that the one person with you was killed. Your job, if you win, will be to protect me. I am starting to feel a little unsafe around you now."

"Well, I hope you wouldn't be in as much trouble as he was. Just don't piss off both the Empire and the Republic, and you should be fine. I doubt you would have enemies that strong against you."

He laughed. "Now I am intrigued. But I have to admit, I had my men search far and wide and there is no record of you on any server. I mean, there are pictures of you, but even they're indicating you don't seem to exist."

I shrugged. "I guess I am good at what I do then."

Kane scooted a little closer to me and placed his arm on the seat behind me. "And what's that?"

"Surviving."

"Now that is what I like to hear. And one of the best ways to survive is to answer my questions back in my office."

"Of course. I was planning on answering them, Mister Hulligan. I'm not one to lie when I see no reason to."

"That's good. I will remember that."

He was quiet the rest of the way while I sipped on my whiskey. Even if it was laced with anything, my powers would just destroy it before it affected anything. Nygard taught me how to do that last month. I doubted it was poisoned though, as he was more of a gentleman than many of the men I knew. Also, he had poured himself a glass as well and was sipping on it gingerly.

We pulled up to the office and the driver let both Kane and I out. He took my hand and placed it around his arm, as if we were going to a ball or something.

"I take it you don't have any weapons on you since you didn't use them against my men."

I smiled. "Smart man. No, I don't have anything."

"Good, then my men don't have to search you."

It surprised me he was so trusting of me. He didn't

know me, but I suppose his deduction led him to believe he was right. A man's cocky nature was his downfall.

He led me up the elevator to the ninety-fifth floor. It was strange being in this building without Jack, as it looked much the same. It was decorated differently, sure, but it still was the same layout and had the same feel to it. Kane apparently liked the color green, as the main entry downstairs was all green, and so was the elevator. Even with such an overuse of the color, this guy wasn't as crazy and probably wouldn't have as many clocks as Jack did in his office, as that was his thing. With my free hand, I checked my pocket. I still had my pocket watch from the future, or the past, depending which way you looked at it. Apparently, it was a gift from my mother— my real mother from Sanshli—and the father that raised me gave it to me before he was murdered right in front of me.

It was all I had of her.

Luckily it was safe, and I was thankful for that. It was something that connected me to my life before, and I needed that. Everything about my life now was crazy, and I didn't care for it. I just wanted a simple life with Jack.

A simple life on Recar.

I shook the thought of a life like that out of my head. There is no way that would happen, I wouldn't be so lucky.

The elevator stopped, and we were let out on the level that held Kane's, and someday Jack's, office. More green lined the hallway, which at least wasn't a bad green. It was like a deep forest green. I glanced around and saw the receptionist table, which was occupied by an amber-haired young lady. Something about these gang leaders and the need to have a pretty receptionist.

"Hello Mister Hulligan." She gave him a smile. "All the files are ready for you on your desk."

"Thank you, Jane." Kane nodded. "Much appreciated."

I wondered what files she could mean. I didn't like it when someone wanted to show me files, as it meant they had found something they shouldn't have.

We entered his office and, not so surprisingly, he had some strange objects he collected. He apparently loved spoons. There were so many of them. They were of all unique styles, some of them had sayings on them, some had different planet commemorative spoons. There was every type of spoon one could think of. After a few moments of inspection, I ignored it. At least they wouldn't create obnoxious sounds every hour like Jack's clocks. Or half an hour.

Kane let go of my hand and pulled back a chair for me. "Take a seat."

I did as he asked as he went around the old wooden desk that I realized Jack also used in the future. How old was this desk? It was less worn than when Jack had it, but it still looked pretty busted. I even recognized some of the blood stains.

This was a well-made desk then.

Kane took a deep breath. "Now, Miss Ryetirf, I want to know, do you know any of the other racers in the event tomorrow?"

I kept a cool composure, even though my heart felt like it was about to jump out of my chest. I shook my head. "No, I never took a look at the list. I mean I might, but to my knowledge, no."

He brought his fingers to a temple as he leaned back. "Interesting. The garage you had your bike in, though, had other cars and people in it."

I shrugged. "Found a good deal where to put my bike, I figured the other guys there were racers, but I don't know them."

Straightening back up, he flipped through one of the files. "Tell me a little bit about yourself, Miss Ryetirf."

"You can call me Myra," I said with a little softness in my tone. I caressed the desk in front of me, looking down at it. "If I will eventually be your driver, you won't need to use such formalities." I figured I would hint that this was a job I wanted, and how we would be close and that would lead him to believe that I wouldn't be lying. I glanced up at him, to see what his reaction was. He had a half smile on his face, which is what I expected.

He let out a chuckle. "You are just full of surprises, aren't you, Myra? First you bite my head off, then you flirt with me in a bar, then disappear for four months. You have any idea how long it took to track you down? It was almost as if you had been off planet for the entire time."

It was my turn to smile. "Maybe I was, maybe I wasn't. As you know, I don't like having that much attention on myself—it attracts the wrong people."

"And am I the right or wrong sort of people?"

I licked my lips. "That will depend on you."

He straightened up and coughed. "You were telling me a bit about yourself, Myra. Where are you from?"

"Far away. A little piece of nowhere. Ever heard of Garvner?"

He raised an eyebrow. "You're from that dump?"

I laughed. "Yes, but I was kidnapped a long, long time ago. I was a prisoner of some greedy people for a while, and then I killed the leader and broke free. That is why I don't quite exist, you see? Because if I made a name for myself, then those who destroyed my life will come after me."

Kane was silent for a moment, as if debating if what I said was true. It explained why I didn't have much paperwork. Garvner wasn't high tech and most of the people there weren't registered in the Galactic Database, not even in the future. Then, if I was kidnapped, no one would have wanted to make real documentation of me.

Kane flipped through the file again and stood up. "I see. What a tough childhood."

I shrugged as he rounded the table towards where I was seated. "It was a long time ago. I am a completely different person now, always on the run, and always getting into some kind of trouble. Having no identity comes in handy for that, I assure you. I could keep you safe, if I win, that is."

He stopped behind me and placed his hands on my shoulders. "Oh, I don't have a doubt in my mind that you will." He paused for a second. "What do you think of Recar?"

"It's entertaining. I feel there would always be something for me to do and I would never get bored."

"Oh, I guarantee you, you wouldn't. Now, as my driver, you know you wouldn't be able to leave Recar, and if you try to leave, my men will kill you on the spot."

I turned to look at him. "I am well aware."

"Good." He grabbed my hand and pulled me up. "I want you to look at this city at its finest and tell me you truly want to stay here."

This is the exact same thing that Jack did the first time I was in his office. He showed me how beautiful the skyline was and tried to get me to be dazzled by it. It didn't work. Well, maybe just a little.

Standing near the window, I looked out at the city. Although this office structure was the tallest building on Recar, most of the buildings were sky-rises and felt dense, although not as dense as Valle. It surprised me that Recar didn't start using flying transports like Valle did, but stuck to the ground with cars and motorbikes. I had a feeling it was because the leader was always afraid that if someone could come up to their level of a building, that it was easier to be assassinated. It made sense.

I took in the view I had seen a hundred times. It made me miss Jack a little and the life we once had. I guess we had a life, but it wasn't the same, nor did I know where it was going. I didn't know how all of this would end up, but I just hoped I would end up together with him.

Nighttime was always beautiful to look at, as all the neon signs and lights of the buildings were on, as if the city never slept. People were crowded on the streets and there were cars as far as the eye could see. It didn't help that a good chunk of the streets on the edge of the city were closed for the race, although I felt that the streets were always this congested. I was glad they had an underground rail system, however, that could get busy.

"It's beautiful."

"I think so too. I wouldn't trade it for any other world."

"Have you been off planet much?" I asked.

"A few times, but not for long. I have a lot of business to take care of here, as you can imagine."

I indeed could.

"Although I admire this view, Mister Hulligan, I need to get back to my hotel and get a good night's sleep before the race tomorrow. Are you done asking the questions you need from me?"

"There are just a few more. I want you to take a look at some contestants and let me know if you recognize them. While I believe you didn't come with any of them, I want you to look, nevertheless."

Leading me back from his desk, he shuffled through some files and took out three. He opened each of them. It was what I expected. He figured out the ones connected to the Empire and Republic. He was smarter than we gave him credit for. Even with all the fake information we made for each of them, he could still trace them back to their true identity.

"Do you know these other three?" He asked me, watching my face closely.

I debated on answering. I had told him I was on the run from everyone, so if he knew anything about these three then he would know who they were. If I had pissed off the wrong people, as I typically did, I would know the face and name of all top officials that would be after me, just to be safe.

Why did I have to say I was on the run from both sides?

I flipped through all photos and information he had found on them. The "fake" names they all used for the races were their names from the future. It made it a lot easier to keep track of it. I looked through the real info he had on them. A lot of it was redacted, but Kane found a lot more than he should have. I wondered if it was because Recar had a lot of hackers, or if Kane knew people in prominent places. I noticed that he had nothing on Jack, which made sense, as he was from this planet and had no ties to either side. I set the files down.

"I have run into these men before, yes. These two." I pointed at Tim and Logan. "Work for the Pandronan Emperor that is making an uproar. I have pissed them off quite a few times, actually. Why they are here, I'm not sure. It could be because they tracked me down to the races, or they could be after you and want to take over this planet for their Empire."

"Good to know. I had my suspicions. They had good fake IDs, but I could find stuff on them. What about the other guy?"

The other guy was one of my brother's crew, Will Basen, who was now General Alan Marc. He and I didn't get along. Our hatred for each other was stronger than the one Tim and I had, which was saying something. I wanted to tell him all about Alan and get him kicked out. It would make my life so much easier, and I just liked to piss him off. I acted dumb though, as I didn't need him coming after me.

"The Second Republic. He's a general or admiral or something along those lines. May or may not have pissed him off as well. He could be here because of you, me, or they heard about the Imperials."

Kane gathered the files and stacked them. "Such honesty. I didn't expect you to tell me all this."

I raised an eyebrow. "Oh? Why not? If I tell you, then you can keep an eye open for me. Better to have more than one person watching my back, I always say."

He traced my spine with his fingers. "Oh, I will watch your back. You just have to promise me you will watch mine."

"Is that a job offer? The races haven't even started."

He chuckled. "Let's just say I can be easily persuaded. Besides, there are many jobs that I can think of for someone with your capabilities."

"You barely know me; how do you know I'm not lying and suck at everything I do?"

He leaned in closer, his face inches from my own. "Well, since most of the words that come out of your mouth are lies, or at least half truths, I would say anyone who is as good as you at lying must be a damn wonderful ally."

Grabbing my hand, he kissed it gently. His eyes met

mine, as if looking for an invitation, which I wouldn't give him. I did not need Jack coming here and beating this guy's ass.

As he let go of my hand, I bit my lip. "Tempting, but how about we make a deal? If I win the races, I'll show you my true worth." I placed my hands on his chest, tracing my finger on the button of his shirt. "And then you and I can discuss the terms of my jobs."

He licked his lips. "I like the sound of that. It's a deal." He leaned forward as if to kiss me. I placed my finger on his lips.

"Ah, ah. Contract first." I kissed his cheek, the scruff of his beard reminding me of Jack. "Until then."

He let out a slow breath. "Let me walk you out?"

"It would be my pleasure."

Chapter 5

So that went better than expected.

I mean, it could have gone a lot worse on my side. He found out about Logan, Tim, and Alan, but I had no idea what he would do about it. If he were smart, which I had a feeling he was, he wouldn't act on anything and wait to see what their first move was. If they were after me, then they would strike. If they were after Kane, he would be ready. If he was wrong though, and acted first, it could bring an entire war to the planet, and I doubted he wanted that.

Either way, I hoped he was wouldn't find more information on me since I knew he would be watching my every move from now on. Now I just had to stay away from the others.

Great.

"What hotel are you staying at, miss?" Kane's driver asked.

I let out a sigh, knowing I would have to stay somewhere new. At least the names of the hotels on Recar hadn't changed. "The Grand."

He nodded and started off towards the hotel. It was a fancy hotel, and I would just have to get a small room. Luckily, I knew the name of the hotel, but I had to worry whether a room was even available. Usually there was, as there were many hotels all around the city, and because this one was pretty pricy. However, with the races going on, I wasn't sure if it would be all booked up or not.

Now, to do the thing I didn't look forward to doing—explaining to Nygard what had just happened. I closed my eyes and focused on communicating with him.

There has been a change in plans. I sent the message through my mind. It was still weird to do this, even after a few months, but it worked and was a lot more convenient than any gadget. No one could trace what we were talking about, or know that I was even talking to someone.

What happened? Are you all right? I could hear his voice in my mind. It surprised me he hadn't tried to communicate with me earlier, as I was late for meeting up with them after dinner. Then again, he knew I wanted to get away for a bit and may have been giving me my space. It wasn't like I was in any actual danger as I was a Sanshlian.

Unless someone killed to where I couldn't heal fast

enough, but that would be tough. No one usually tried that hard. They would have to stab me in the heart or cut off my head or something like that.

Yes, but I have caught the attention of the leader here and I have a feeling he will be watching me. He figured out I don't exist—at least not in this timeline.

Understood. Where are you heading?

To The Grand Hotel. I will just be staying there for the time being.

We will stay in communication throughout the races. Once this is over, we will revisit your lessons on not catching people's attention.

But isn't it more fun this way?

He didn't answer. It was strange having an overprotective father like him. My father on Garvner was overprotective, but that was when I was young. After he died, I didn't have anyone looking out for me until now. It was strange, I had always been on my own, other than with Jack, but those were rare occasions. We rarely got involved with each other's work unless we had to.

That is until I was looking for Sanshli and Jack tagged along. I guess that was because Emperor Neil threatened him to join, and he was reporting every move to him. Then he betrayed me. He was just trying to do what he thought would help me, though, so I couldn't blame him. There was too much at stake.

Now there was even more at stake.

The gem that we hid in the trophy was the only way of finding Sanshli. I got scolded for four months straight about putting it in the trophy in the first place and the slim possibility someone might find it or somehow tamper with the information on it. I doubted I damaged it, and it was in the safest place throughout all the galaxy. I needed the time to figure out what to do, not to mention I did it before I found out Dan was Nygard. I don't know if I would have changed my mind if knew of his actual identity beforehand or not. There were just too many variables now. I had too much to think about already.

Nygard and I had grown closer in the past four months as he taught me all I needed to know about being a Sanshlian and preparing me to be as strong as him. He needed us to go to Sanshli now to finish the ceremony, and we both could have the most powerful spell of them all—immortality.

And once that happened, I would become more powerful than even him, and this will all be over.

The driver stopped in front of the hotel and as he opened the door for me, he handed me a slip of paper. "This is the location of your motorbike tomorrow. I wish you the best in the races."

I took the paper. "Thank you."

He bowed and closed the door behind me. Glancing at the paper, I found a different address than the garage it was at before. I wondered if he moved it so I wouldn't have to interact with those who had their cars in that garage. Maybe he thought I was in danger being around them and was helping me out.

Or he thought I was up to something and was seeing if I would still try to get in contact with the Imperials.

Moving my bike would make it much harder.

Looking up at the hotel, I found the same old building standing there. It was tall, but still only half the height of the leader's office building. It was made of beige brick with blue and yellow neon lights spelling out "The Grand". I wondered how many times they had to replace those bulbs over the years. They always looked new.

I sighed and entered the hotel to book a room. I neither had my gear or clothes and wasn't sure how I would get either. I guess the only way was to talk to Jack and have him use his connections on this planet.

Yes, even though he wasn't the boss, I knew he had connections.

The interior, like the name of the hotel, was rather grand. The walls were painted a deep blue with rather fancy curtains at the windows, a crystal chandelier, and there was even a large water feature. It was fancy, even though this wasn't close to being the most expensive hotel in the city.

I stepped up to the check-in booth and asked for a single room. The concierge was a tall man with jet black hair that was cut close to his head. He looked awkward, almost like a teenager. I wondered if this was just a part-time job while he went to school, if he even went to school. A lot of these kinds on this planet didn't.

He swiped a card and handed it to me. "Room 1623. Up the elevator and on to the right."

"Thank you."

I headed up the elevator which was also blue on the inside. This place seemed to pick one color theme and stuck to it. I liked this blue better than Kane's green, though. Both were better than the gray rooms I was used to.

I got off floor 16 and swiped open the door to my room. It was a typical room with one bed, kitchenette, TV, and bathroom set-up that was in most hotels. Again, the walls were blue with yellow accents, which was magnified from the light of the neon sign that was radiating into the room. I sat down on the bed and took a deep breath. I had only been on this planet for a few hours and so much had already happened.

Typical for this planet.

I fell back, letting my spine relax on the bed. The other reason I picked this hotel was for the comfy beds. They always made my back feel so much better. I lay there for a few moments, trying to destress and decide what I would do next.

First things first, though—I needed my stuff.

I could have Nygard send it to me, but I didn't want Kane to find out I had any connection with the Imperials. They would be watching. Good thing Jack would stay at his own apartment versus with my brother.

Hey, Jack.

What is it, my love?

I explained everything that had happened with Kane and how he knew about Tim, Logan, and Jane. I even told him how I could get away and flirted with him to get on his good side. I didn't feel like hiding any of it from Jack since he would get pissed when he found out after reading my mind. I also wanted him to stay away from my brother and his friends as much as he could since Kane was keeping an eye on them as well. It would look fishy is Jack was seen with them.

After a moment, Jack answered. *I'm gonna kill him.*

I knew you would say that. But also, you were no different when I started in the races.

Exactly, I know all the thoughts that are going through his head and what he wants to do with you.

I can take care of myself, Jack.

I know, but that doesn't mean I'm okay with any of it.

You don't have to be. Besides, it's not like we are staying here. We just need to get the gem and get out of here, all right? Focus on that for the time being.

Fine, I will, but only because I know no other man can have you except me.

Whatever makes you happy. Now then, I need you to do me a favor.

Anything for you.

I rolled my eyes. He and Kane were two peas in a pod. It was ridiculous. *I need you to get some clothes and weapons to me. I don't want to ask Nygard for the ones I brought because I don't want Kane finding our connection.*

Sure, I can pick some things out for you and send an IK.

An IK, or Information Kid. It had been a while since I had used one. They were orphans who lived off selling information, transferring small goods, and any odd job. Jack explained to me he used them a lot more than many of the other mob bosses because he used to be one, until the previous leader saw his toughness, adopted him, and made him his successor. It was strange to think of Jack as being anything but a crime lord. I couldn't imagine him a kid living off the streets.

You should get a knock at your door in the next hour. And I will pick out some clothes especially for you.

Just my normal style clothes, Jack. I don't need to raise suspicion. Also, I need a jumpsuit, black if you can find it. Bulletproof too.

Yes ma'am.

I opened my eyes and stared at the simple white ceiling, seeing if I could make up images from the random spots and dents. The only things I were seeing were a milkshake, potatoes, apples, and any other food I could think of. My stomach growled.

Maybe I was getting hungry.

Getting up, I rang the food service number and ordered their special, which was a butternut squash and sage risotto. It sounded delicious and if the food here was anything like what it was in the future, it would be spectacular.

The restaurant in the hotel said it would be about a half hour, so I stepped into the shower and tried to process everything that had happened and what would happen.

I let the hot water consume me as I stood in the shower. It felt good to have actual water pouring on me, as the ship we used to travel from Anosira didn't have a proper shower. I let it relax my body before using their complimentary shampoo.

Kane didn't suspect me of anything other than keeping secrets. I was a mystery, and very few people were. I also had this theory that all the leaders here wanted to sleep with every single woman of their choosing who were on this planet, like it was some kind of conquest checklist. At least after Jack and I met, I knew he had given up that conquest game, as he knew I would kill any woman that tried to take him from me.

It was strange to think that Jack was no longer the leader of Recar. I wasn't even sure if he would get that life back once we found Sanshli. I wasn't sure if we would even venture back to the future, or if we would be stuck at this point in time. Maybe we went back into the past when Nygard was first encased in the stone. I had asked Jack about it, and he always shrugged it off, like it wasn't important. I found it to be important as I wanted my life back before this entire mess even happened.

Or, at least, part of my life.

I didn't want to go back to working for Emperor Neil, as he didn't care for me nor I him. More than anything, I just wanted to live my life with Jack on this planet. In the future, where he ruled this place. Or better yet, we could both just run away and hide from everything. That sounded like the best scenario, but we already had that discussion months ago and we decided it wouldn't work, as Nygard or someone else would find us. They always did.

I shut the water off and dried myself with a towel. I realized then that I didn't have any clean clothes to change into. Luckily there were a couple of robes in the closet and I put one of them on and waited for room service to show up.

I had nothing to keep myself occupied, and I wasn't one for watching mindless television, but I turned it on anyway, even if just for the background noise. I figured it would look strange if I was just sitting here with nothing going on when the room service came. Turning on the TV, news about previous races was playing. I guess I might as well see what had happened in the history of the races, as if I didn't know.

A couple of moments later, a knock on the door made me jump a little and someone on the other side said, "Room service."

I opened the door and a man who appeared similar to the kid at the front desk wheeled in a silver cart with a plate covered with a metal lid.

"Please enjoy your meal and let us know if you need anything else." The man bowed and left me to my meal.

I took off the metal lid and steam came lofting off of the risotto. I was about drooling, ready to have my meal in peace. I had to eat with other people normally, something I didn't enjoy, so this was a pleasant change of pace for me.

Scarfing down the meal, I relished every bite. I definitely would order it again if it stayed on the special list for a while. Sitting down on the bed, I finished watching the report on the previous races. All the record times were a lot lower than when I had raced, so I doubted I would have any problem being victorious. If I could win once, I knew I would do it again. There was no doubt in my mind.

There was a silent tap at the door, and I rushed over to

open it. A boy that went up to about my hip was standing there with two enormous bags.

"Miss Ryetirf, ma'am?" the boy asked.

"Yes."

"These are for you," he tried to lift the bags but had some trouble as they were about the same size as him.

I grabbed the bags. "Thank you." I slipped him some cash, and he ran off to wherever he would hang out the rest of the night. I closed the door and dumped the contents of the bags onto the bed.

Jack did as I asked and only got me my typical clothes: black tanks, jeans, or cargo pants, and boots. He also got me an all-black jumpsuit. The only choice of mine he decided to alter was the bra and underwear. I held up the thong and shook my head.

I was going to kill him.

Chapter 6

Today was the big day. Or at least the start of the big days to come, as this was a four-day event.

The streets were lined with people, even though they were advised to stay inside to watch the races since accidents did happen. I couldn't blame them, though. I would want to watch what was happening with my own eyes too. Then again, I could heal myself if anything happened and these people, to the best of my knowledge, could not.

I could hear both applause and cussing coming at me while riding my motorbike. Someone racing with a motorbike had never happened in all the history of the races, no one had even done it in the future. I wondered how Nygard was able to get them to let me race with it, and whether he used his powers of persuasion to do it.

Either way, I was getting what I wanted, and I was very thankful for that. I just hoped that I could succeed and not get run over. I had been cocky about not letting anyone catches up to me before, but then I thought about the fact that Tim, Logan, and Alan were all racing, and they would use this opportunity to run me over if they could, not to mention they had powers and could use those to their advantage.

It would be a very interesting race. I could barely hold in my excitement. I was thankful that no one could see under my helmet as they would make fun of my giant smile. It was rare for me to show a smile, or at least a genuine one.

I glanced around for Jack, wondering where he was among all these cars. The order of the cars was selected by random, and my bike was right in the middle, which would be fun. I could already tell the two cars next to me were conspiring to crush me the first chance they got. I couldn't wait to zoom past them when the light turned green.

Where are you? I asked Jack through our mind connection. *I can't tell which car is yours.*

Take another look around and guess.

I looked around again and saw a car with a clock painted on it. I took a deep breath. *Oh wow, Jack, you have a problem.*

I just wanted you to be able to spot me if need be. Also, you are going to get killed on that bike of yours.

I laughed. *As if. I will show you once and for all that motorbikes are better than cars.*

If you say so.

Besides, I can't die, or at least not easily.

I'm glad that is your backup plan—the fact you are some alien from Sanshli with magical powers.

You know me, I will take any advantage that I can get.

You mean like seducing the leader of this planet?

I told you nothing happened.

He tried to kiss you.

Which is typical for any man on this planet. Now focus, Jack, the race is about to start.

Workers were getting off of the track and out of the way so that the cars could start their engines. I switched on my motorbike and got in a ready stance. The countdown light blinked red.

Oh, Cadi?

Yes?

Are you wearing the underwear I picked out?

The light turned green, and I almost didn't hit the gas.

You son of a bitch!

I raced past his stupid car and made a gesture showing him how I felt about it. And yes, I was wearing it since it was all I had.

It was easy to get in the front as my motorbike could accelerate quicker with a smaller mass. It was also a little modified to go faster than any motorcycle on the market.

I noticed that while riding it last night. I made sure this morning it hadn't been tampered with by Kane's men. I half expected him to do something, as I had learned to never trust anyone. I didn't even trust Jack completely, though that was more for things like picking out my clothes.

It was not comfortable to ride like this, so I would definitely be stopping at a store for some other underwear tonight.

How are you doing? I heard father's voice come into my mind. Usually he didn't communicate with me until I reached out to him, so it threw me off a little.

Everything is going good on my side. If you don't see, I'm in first place right now.

I do see that. Tim and Logan are in fifth and seventh. Seems Jack is in second and Alan is in sixth.

I figured Jack would be second, as he was the only one out of the group that knew the roads even better than me. *Sounds like one of us has an excellent chance in getting first, and that someone is me.*

Don't get too cocky, daughter, I wouldn't put it past the others to use a dirty trick.

Oh, I'm counting on it. Don't worry, I'm prepared for anything.

Fine, show me what you've got.

I pushed on the gas a little more and the motorcycle felt as if it was soaring through the air. I enjoyed racing on this bike compared to the car I used in the past. I couldn't wait to prove to Jack I was right and make him eat his words.

Or crash and have him make me eat my words.

I didn't know what I would do if I crashed. It would mean I would be disqualified as I wouldn't have a vehicle to drive with. Nygard must have trusted me a lot to believe I could win this race with a bike and not get into a nasty accident. I had to live up to his expectations and not screw up.

No pressure or anything.

I rounded the next corner and found myself on the very edge of the city where I could see the roaring sea below the roadway. It crashed against the rocky cliff, sending water up onto the roadway. I timed it just right so I didn't get hit by the water, not wanting to get wet or slip. In a car it would be fine, as Jack proved behind me as his car got hit, but in a motorbike, I would have to be careful on that turn. I took a mental note of that.

The next part of the roadway was a mix of tunnels, sharp pin turns, and I would be onto the next lap. The tunnel was loud, even being in first. I could hear the main cars behind me as the sound echoed along the walls. It was exhilarating.

I could not wait to see what else would be in store for the next day's race.

I passed the line and entered the second lap. There was always three laps for each race. I glanced in my little mirror on my handlebars to find Jack and another car gaining up on me. Jack must have modified his car. It was stupid of them to use the boosters on the second lap, when it was the third lap that really mattered.

The fronts of their cars were on either side of me and I swerved a bit to get away from the one that wasn't Jacks, as he was trying to hit me with the front of his car. The jerk had very poor sportsmanship. I pushed the gas more, but they could keep up with me.

As we rounded a corner, I saw a large ocean wave

coming towards the corner. I slowed down, hoping I would time it just right. As the larger wave washed over the two cars, more than likely causing them both to lose vision for a moment, I was able to weave past them and back into first.

Take that, Jack.

Cheap trick.

It wasn't me; it was nature coming to support me.

Whatever, I bet you controlled the wave to do that.

Nope, it wasn't. I'm just lucky.

Well, I don't mind you in front. I will just sit back and enjoy the view.

Shut up.

He had a point though, I could use the wave to my advantage later if I needed. I could also use my powers to make sure I wouldn't get hit by the water. Sometimes, when one focuses too much at the task at hand, they forget all the advantages they had.

And I had a lot of advantages.

The last tunnel was easy and people cheered as I started lap three. Glancing behind me, I saw Jack was still on my tail. I smiled, knowing he had an ace up his sleeve and thought he would get the better of me. This technically was the easiest level of the four races. It was also the shortest, sort of like a taste of what all the other levels would be like.

I was excited to see what else lay in store for us.

From my knowledge of the races, the laps were different with each tournament. I mean, they had to reuse some layouts as there have been many, many tournaments throughout the centuries, as it was held every time a driver of the mob boss was killed or fired, though if they were fired they were probably killed in some weird accident not too long after. Either way, there had to have been over a hundred races held when I won to get close to Jack.

It wasn't always the first-place winner that got the job offer, but they got the gold trophy they could melt down and feed their family for the rest of their lives. Usually they took the job offer, if it was given, since they wouldn't want the mob mad at them. Sometimes the job was offered to the second or third winner, depending on sportsmanship, type of driving, etc. The leader didn't want someone who was haphazard in the way they drove, even if it meant they were the fastest.

It was strange to see the streets so empty in the front, especially when Recar was always full of traffic. It was nice, and I wished I could drive like this whenever I was on the planet. I also liked not getting chased down by cops, or the equivalent of cops here, if I was breaking the traffic laws. Or just getting chased in general.

Then again, I had an entire line of cars behind me.

The time for everyone to use the boosters that no one cared were illegal was here. Checking back again, more cars were gaining up on me. I wondered which car was Alan, as I knew he would try his best to hit me. Although, I presumed all these cars except for Jack wanted to hit me.

That made it even more fun.

I didn't have time to put more mods on my

motorcycle, but I also found it to be cheating. It was not cheating, however, to use a bit of my powers to make sure I get first. I focused on my wheels and used my powers to make them go a little faster.

The thrill of making this motorbike go even faster was intoxicating. Now I always wanted to go this fast, but knew there was no way the bike could handle it for a lengthy period of time, and I didn't want to raise any suspicion.

As I saw the cars behind me lose distance, I stopped using my powers. There was no way they could make up that difference now. Unless one of the others used their powers. They didn't have powers that could help them like I did, as I could control anything I wanted with my Illusionist powers, where theirs were just elemental.

Which was why the Illusionists were treated like demons on Sanshli.

My father and his people were spit upon, and their ancestry and powers taken away from them. It was why he rebelled; it was why he killed so many of the Sanshlians. It made sense, and I didn't see him as much as the monster that my mother and the stories made him out to be.

But he still killed them all and caused chaos throughout the entire galaxy.

I shook my head. It was not the time to focus on that.

Coming up to the spot where the water washed on the street, I took a deep breath and commanded the wave to calm down as I passed. I could feel the ocean—it felt like an entity all on its own, as if angry at this world for always being so rainy and gloomy. It wanted to be a free spirit and escape. The sea here wasn't something revered or celebrated like it was on Anosira. On Anosira, everyone wanted to go to the beach, feel the warm sand and waves on their skin, but here it was cold, with strong currents that could sweep you under. There were rarely any sandy areas, but just rocky cliffs. No one wanted to go near it.

I could understand this ocean.

I was able to calm it for a moment as I passed the spot and let it go on in being the strong, free entity it wanted to be. I had a feeling the wave behind me would be even stronger, as it had all the pent-up rage. Glancing behind me, I saw a giant wave crash over the street, causing one car to swerve and hit the side of the barrier. All the other cars went around the wave and it surprised me none of the others crashed into it. They must have been professionals this year. Sometimes that wasn't always the case.

Okay, that was on purpose. Jack said in my mind.

A girl will never tell.

Whatever, you are lucky you didn't cause an even worse crash. You could have hurt me, you know.

Ah, I knew you would be okay.

With all that commotion, I was leading but a lot more now and knew there would be no way someone would pass me, unless there was some kind of accident. I doubted any of my brother's group would use their powers on me this early in the game, but made a note to look out for anything the others might be up to.

I went through the tunnel, coming out to hear cheering as I went over the finish line. Fireworks sprang up from the buildings and lit up the clouds above us.

"The motorcyclist did it! She won first place!"

One race down, three more to go.

Chapter 7

There was so much shit to deal with when one was competing in the races. Shit I didn't want to deal with.

First there were the interviews, which I did because I didn't care if anyone saw my face this time. I kept all my answers short. They tried to dig for different information, but I didn't give them any. They also tried to see if I had any involvement with the other racers. I said I didn't and left it at that. Journalists were always so pushy with their questions, and I hated it.

Then I had to take my bike in to get it cleaned up and tuned up. I doubted it needed too much work, but I figured I would be safe rather than sorry. Luckily, I didn't have to find someone and hope they wouldn't try to sabotage it as Kane hired me a mechanic. He waiting for me when I got to the garage. He was a short, skinny boy with freckles that were covered in grease marks. He had to be about the same age as me—young to be a mechanic. However, if Kane had sent him, I knew he was good.

"Wow you really rode hard on this bike. I haven't seen tires worn down this bad in a long time." The boy rolled over some new tires. I wanted to comment that no one could wear tires like I had since I had used my powers to get the bike to go faster than it was used to.

"Well you don't see many bikes used for the races, I'm sure," I said.

He chuckled. "Yeah, I suppose. It will be a pleasure working on this bike, miss. I haven't had a project this fun in years."

I wondered how many years he could mean, but I didn't ask. It was always surprising how early kids on this planet started working and apprenticing under someone. I thought that was a better way to work versus going to school since it was a lot more direct. Besides, it wasn't like these kids would miss any life lessons along the way—Recar was a hard planet to live on as it was.

I stayed and watched him work on my bike. Although Kane had sent him, I didn't trust anyone not to do something to my bike. I leaned back against the wall and watched the boy go to work. He didn't say much, but was hyper-fixated on making sure everything was perfect for the race tomorrow. It was impressive.

There were a couple of other cars in here, but they weren't for the races. I wondered if this was Kane's personal garage as there were some nice-looking cars. I guess if Kane wanted to sabotage my bike, he could do it while I wasn't here, but I ignored that fact. I just had to trust him.

I took a closer look at the cars as the mechanic finished up with the bike. There were five other cars that were all black with tinted windows. Glancing inside, I found that they all had minibars.

Yup, these were definitely Kane's cars.

As if thinking about the devil made him appear, I heard Kane's voice come from the entrance.

"Myra, my favorite driver, how is my mechanic doing?"

I turned to find him smiling with about six armed men with him.

"He's doing a marvelous job. I think he's almost done even."

The mechanic held up his hand. "Give me five minutes and I will be finished."

Kane smiled. "You are an angel, Dennis."

Dennis. So that was his name. He never said it and I couldn't read the faded nametag he had on. I doubted it would matter.

"Do you make it your job to check up on all the racers, or am I just special?" I asked as he stepped towards me.

He opened his arms up as if shrugging. "What can I say, I like to invest in things that I deem worthy."

More flirting. Typical. "Well, I am honored."

He gestured to the cars. "These are more the type of cars you will be driving, although I do want to ride with you on that motorbike sometime. Seems like a lot of fun."

"They are nice cars, I will admit. I noticed they all have minibars in them as well."

He laughed. "Well, I always like to entertain my guests. It is unfortunate you won't be able to have anything, though, as you will be driving. I guess there is always after we get back to the office."

"I suppose there is."

"Done!" Dennis shouted, raising his arms. It impressed me he was so quick. He really was a genius, I could see why Kane kept him around. His smile so wide that he had dimples on each cheek. Kane ruffled his hair.

"That's a good mechanic. Now, your mom said she was almost ready for supper. You better head home."

"Thank you, sir!" he said as he hurried towards the door. That was rather… pure. So he must have been a couple of years younger than me. I wondered how long he has been working on cars then.

"Tomorrow's races will be harder, as you probably know from your research." Kane turned to me.

I nodded. "Of course. I'm looking forward to it."

"I don't know how well your bike will handle the laps we have prepared, but I am excited to see you take up the challenge."

"I wouldn't have it any other way, sir. I always love a good challenge."

"And a good challenge you shall have this tournament. Each race will get a bit harder and I have some fun things in store for the final round. I hope none of the other races hurt you in the process."

"I can take care of myself, don't worry."

He let up a half smile. "I bet you can." He tapped his cane on the ground. "As for the Imperial and Republic racers, they seemed to be doing good as well. The Imperials got third and seventh and the Republic third. Any of them could get extra points in the next race and pass you up."

I shook my head. "Not possible, I don't intend on losing any of the races. I have to show my worth, after all."

He paused, as if taking in all the conversations we had ever had. "What are you going to do if they come after you?"

I blinked, surprised at the question. "Excuse me?"

"If those three are actually after you and not here for some other reason, are you just going to run away and leave this planet? Or are you going to stay?"

I bit my lip. He thought I would bail after the races. I mean, I was going to since we were just trying to get the gem and go to Sanshli. I couldn't explain that though, nor did I want to upset him with what was going on behind his back.

"If they are after me, none of them have jurisdiction in this area, and I hope the leader in this area will have my back when I defend myself."

He smiled. "That is what I like to hear. You have my blessing to protect yourself, of course. I wouldn't want any harm to come to my future driver."

"If I win the races. You keep forgetting that part," I added.

He shrugged. "I doubt you will lose. Besides, you don't

have to get first for me to pick you."

I put my hand on his shoulder as I started towards the door. "Don't get ahead of yourself, Kane. You never know what will happen in the future."

I left him standing there, as I wanted to grab dinner. Kane mentioning that Dennis' mother had supper ready reminded me I wanted to see if my hotel was making risotto again.

The hotel wasn't too far from where the garage was, which was nice as I didn't have to go down to the Underground and deal with that busy mess. I peered around at all the citizens who were going on with their day, trying to catch up after having watched the race. No one seemed to care about the surrounding people, just paying attention to themselves and what they believed was important.

It felt so disconnected, but at the same time I knew I was disconnected from the worlds when I was the Emperor's Shadow. There was so much to each of the planets, but it seemed like no one cared and they just did what they needed to survive.

Was that what I was like, only doing what I needed to survive and didn't take in the world around me? I supposed I was.

With these powers I was learning to use, it felt like I could almost feel everything around me. It was something I liked to keep turned off most of the time or I would lose track of what I was doing. I took a deep breath. I was still learning, and one day I could use it at all times and be able to take it all in.

The feeling told me I was being watched. I tried to reach out to see who it was, but I still wasn't powerful enough to figure out who or what it was. I kept a note on it, though, to make sure it wasn't a threat. The person could just be a journalist trying to get information. Or maybe I was wrong, and I was just so used to being watched that I was making it up.

I could be wrong though.

Going forward, I made my way to the hotel. Once I was there, I knew the person couldn't follow me up to my room. The hotels here were rather secure, which was surprising. I guess there had to be somewhere on this planet that people could be safe.

I headed straight towards the restaurant and asked what the specials were. The man said that they still had some risotto, and I ordered it to be delivered to my room. I didn't care for eating alone at a table and wanted to be by myself since I could.

It was great that I got separated from the others. I could finally relax and not want to punch someone.

Getting up to my room, I collapsed on the bed and focused on talking to Nygard to do my daily check in. He wanted me to check in with him since he was now a little paranoid after the fiasco with Kane the night before. I couldn't blame him, but he didn't know this planet like I did. It was the norm.

Everything is fine on my end. What about yours?

We are doing good. We are trying to figure out what the track will be tomorrow so Tim and Logan will have a better chance to get higher rankings and beat the Republic's chance of getting the trophy.

Figuring out the track is near impossible here as they do a superb job of hiding that info. Heck, I don't think they decide it until tomorrow. Besides, I'm doing well and doubt I will lose. You guys need not worry.

I'd rather have a backup plan in case anything happens. But yes, you did good. Jack was a close second though and I fear you are a little too connected to him. He could be using you.

He definitely wasn't.

He just wants to help me, father, he won't ruin your plan.

Be careful who you trust, I made the same mistake a long time ago.

Nygard was talking about my mother, Violet. He had loved her so much, yet she didn't follow him when he rebelled against their race. I could understand his frustration and not wanting to trust anyone.

I understand. I won't make that mistake.

Good. I'll talk to you tomorrow. If anything comes up, please contact me.

I will.

With that, I felt the connection fade away. A moment later, there was a knock at the door. My food was here.

Chapter 8

With a happy stomach, I decided to take a shower and wind down for the night. The hot water felt good on my skin as I rinsed off the soap. Thankfully, I remembered to get new underwear down the street before stepping in the shower. I had to remember to punch Jack later for that.

I put on the pajamas, which were comfortable. Since they were men's lounge pants with a black shirt, they were actually Jack's own pajamas, and he clearly wanted me to wear them.

I sat down on the bed and wondered if I should contact him or not. I knew if I did, that he would make his way over, and I didn't want to draw attention to myself regarding Kane. I felt he was always watching closely, especially since he kept appearing, just like Jack used to.

Though, I was curious about what was going on with my brother Rik and the others. His name was Wesley Atkins in this life, the ruler of the Second Republic. I wondered how he was able to get here without raising suspicion. I guessed he did the same thing I did when we were on Cisum. All the P.A.E., or Pirates Against Empire, knew my face and I could get through the planet for a while before anyone noticed.

The thought of the P.A.E. was strange, as they didn't quite exist yet, and if my brother had anything to say about it, they would never need to exist again. He wanted the Empire never to come back to power, which made sense in his eyes—they were the reason he and I had suffered so much.

The problem I had with him was that he was using tactics that were not legal or moral and mimicked what he said he was fighting against. I found it ironic and decided I would not let him go through with it.

That was how I ended up with Joss again. And how I met Nygard.

I don't doubt that Nygard knew where I was for the year we were getting settled in this new era. He was powerful and a lot different from I ever thought he would be. I trained under him, acted like I wanted to help Joss, but then Tim pissed me off and I ran away. Luckily, I somehow found Jack in all that mess and he and I came up with the plan to put the gem in the trophy for safe keeping.

As I took a deep breath, a knock on the door startled

me.

I stared at the door, as if it was some strange entity. Who could it be? I reached for my TG-2.

Another knock. "Room service."

I hadn't ordered anything else, so either it was a wrong room or whoever was on the other side of the door was a liar. I held the gun behind my back. "Coming!"

I peered out the peephole to see a man dressed in an all blue suit—just like the rest of the workers in this hotel. He was either legit or had stolen the outfit. There was only one way to find out.

Opening the door, I watched as the young man smiled, wheeling the cart with the silver platter into the room. He was either fantastic at acting or was just a naïve boy who worked here. At this point I was going with the latter, especially since it seemed like only naïve boys worked at places like this, and apparently as mechanics.

He pulled off the cover of the food. "White chocolate cake, drizzled with a strawberry liquor, and a bottle of blackberry honey wine."

I stared at it, my stomach acting as if it hadn't just eaten the risotto. Well, it was something I would order. I turned to the boy and smiled. "Thank you."

"Just roll the cart in the hallway and we will take care of it. Have a good night." He did a slight bow and left. I was left there, staring at the food, wondering who could have ordered it.

"Did you figure it out yet?"

I pointed my gun down at the cart where Jack had just

rolled out from underneath. I put the gun away.

"Damn it, Jack! I almost shot you!" I couldn't believe he had snuck in under the cart. Of everything he had done in the past, this shouldn't have been as surprising as it was. "How did he not notice the extra weight?"

Jack stood up and smiled. "Oh, he knew I was there. I told him I wanted to surprise the woman I loved." Jack held up a rose. "I can be quite persuasive."

I rubbed my forehead with a small smile on my lips. "Well I guess I'm glad you aren't a killer, but that kid is an idiot for letting you do that. You could be some pervert or something. Although, if we are honest…"

"Hey! I came here because you said we couldn't be seen together. Speaking of which, I noticed you were with him at the garage…"

I let out a small laugh. "So it was you who was following me after I left the garage. I guess that is one worry I don't have to dwell on."

He wrapped his arms around me. "You didn't answer my question, Cadi."

"Because I don't see the problem of talking to some guy on some planet that means nothing," I said with a little smugness in my voice. I knew it was eating him up inside.

He narrowed his eyes. "Well, I didn't like how you easily you could flirt with him in that bar a few months back."

I sighed. "You mob bosses are all alike when you look for women. You want mysterious, strong, and someone you can't charm that easily. I didn't have to try hard,

Jack."

He mumbled. "Yeah, well, that doesn't mean I can't be mad about it."

I shrugged. "Suit yourself, I'm just telling you how it is. I don't feel anything for him. He is just a means to an end."

Giving me his best pouty face. "And what about me? Am I just a means to an end?"

I wrapped my arms around his neck. "You are anything but a means to an end. Or at, least in the current moment."

He laughed then kissed me. "You should eat. I bet you haven't even had dinner."

"First off, you weren't following me that closely as I got some food on my way up. Second, they serve a fantastic butternut and sage risotto here that I would die for. It is probably the best I have ever had."

"I'll make a note that you like risotto. I presume you prefer the vegetarian kind, since I don't think I have ever seen you eat meat."

I shrugged as I took the cake over to the small two-chaired table. "Don't care for it, no, but I can't say I don't eat meat. If the Emperor gave me a meal with some, I would eat it with no comment."

"Mhmm."

"What's that that supposed to mean? You know I'm not loyal to him—not anymore."

"Cadi, I don't know who or what you are loyal to. I just know that I can trust you for a fun time."

"Gee, thanks." Although his words stung a little, he

had an excellent point. I was secretive, a liar, and did whatever I could to achieve my ends. He had no reason to trust me, yet he always did.

We sat down and Jack poured the honey wine into two glasses. "I know you like hard liquor, but I figured this would be a lot smoother for having to race tomorrow."

"I'm not you, Jack, I can hold my liquor, not to mention I know when to stop."

"Touché, my love. Either way, this is a really good bottle and I don't want to waste it."

He handed me a glass, and I took a sip. He wasn't wrong, it was rather delicious. I never had wine like this before.

"What do you call this? He said honey wine, but it doesn't taste like wine."

"It's actually called 'mead'. The kid didn't know that because he isn't old enough to drink, although that doesn't stop anyone here, now does it?"

I laughed. "No, this planet just makes rules for people like us to break them."

He raised his glass. "Exactly. I wouldn't have it any other way. It makes it more exciting, don't you think?"

"Yeah, I suppose it does."

I took a bite of the cake and felt like I was in heaven. It was rich, but not too rich, and tasted almost like warm brownie dough, but with white chocolate instead of cacao. I would be ordering this again.

"You could make that face more often for me, you know."

I shot him a look and took another bite. "Don't ruin my

meal. I'm trying to enjoy this."

"Am I not enjoyable?"

I rolled my eyes and finished my half of the piece. With all his jokes though, he was a great partner to have. He was always there for me, had my back, saved my life quite a few times, and even risked everything he made on this planet to help me. I didn't feel I deserved him.

"Thank you." I whispered. "For… everything."

At first he looked surprised, his eyes wide, but then they softened. "Anything for you, Cadi."

We finished our meal and Jack, for some reason, had a bag of herbal tea in his pocket to make. Luckily there was a teapot in the room he could use. He seemed so elegant while pouring the tea, almost as if he was some proper royalty. He drank a lot of tea since I had known him, and all types too. I had never met someone who had such a passion for tea—although I never got to know someone as closely as I did him.

He set the cups on the small table and sat next to me on the couch. We sat there in silence, and I leaned my head on his shoulder, his warmth feeling comforting against my cheek. Jack caressed my hand, and I watched his rough fingers move back and forth. This was the only thing better than being alone. Everything I ever wanted was right here.

"What are you thinking about?" I asked him. He just laughed.

"Thinking about how great it is to see you again. I just wish it could last forever."

"Maybe it will," I whisper. "Maybe I can find a way for

this to be our eternity."

He moved back so he could look at my face. "You don't mean what I think you mean, do you?"

I shrugged. "I mean, imagine the power that I could control on Sanshli. I could make it so no one ever finds us again and we can just find some corner of the universe to be happy. Is that so wrong?"

He studied me for a long bit, then kissed my forehead. "The fact you want me there is the best thing I have ever heard, Cadi, but you know as well as I that all of this is bigger than we could ever understand."

I leaned against him again, not sure how to take that comment. I would think he would just want to be together, and that finding a way to do that would be ideal for him. Did my brother put stupid ideas in his head? Did he try to tell him how the Sanshlians—the Illusionists—were monsters? That I was a monster? No, I never would believe that Jack would see me as anything but his love, but the comment still resonated in my mind.

Maybe my father was right; maybe I shouldn't trust anyone.

Chapter 9

It was the second day of the races. The crowd was even larger than it had been the day before. I guess the idea of a motorcyclist winning was enough to pique everyone's interest. Lucky me.

Jack had left my room early this morning to get ready. He used one of the service elevators he knew the codes for so Kane's men wouldn't spot him. How he even knew the codes, I had no idea. Even centuries in the past, Jack knew this city in and out.

I was in the front of the lineup this time, as I had won first in the last round. I had to make sure this time I accelerated faster than those around me and not let Jack distract me. If I stuttered even just a little, it would mean that the cars behind me would have time to not only pass me but also try to knock me down. I couldn't let them have that satisfaction, especially since I knew Alan was in third and ready to do just that. Probably Tim and Logan as well, who were just behind him.

Focus on the race, don't let anyone distract you this time. Nygard's voice became clear into my mind. He was referring to Jack.

I will be fine. Don't worry, I've got this in the bag.

So you say. Nothing is guaranteed until the last race is finished. Presuming the future is a mistake I don't want you to make.

That made sense. No one knew the future, not even him. At least, not yet. *I will keep that in mind.*

Good, now get ready. It looks like the race is about to start.

The light blinked red as the crews got off the racetrack. I revved my engine and counted down: 3… 2… 1…

The light turned green, and I pressed on the gas. No one could pass me in the first few seconds, which was a good and bad. I wouldn't get hit right away and I had the lead, which was good, but that meant I would be the first to find out if there were any strange obstacles in this race.

Maybe I should let Jack take the lead for a bit.

I shook my head. No, I couldn't let him have that satisfaction. I would just have to figure this all out myself.

Usually the second race didn't have many obstacles, but was just a little longer than the first race. If it had anything, it would just be on the same level of hazards as the waves washing on the roadway which I was able to work through pretty easily. I would still keep my eyes open though, as I wouldn't put it past Kane to do something flashy.

The first part of the race was a tunnel. If I knew this city like I thought I did, we were going the opposite way we did yesterday. That didn't mean the whole track would be reversed, it was just the first bit. I quickly had to take a pin turn that wasn't in the first race. My bike could handle it fine, but by the sound of tires screeching behind me, it wasn't the easiest thing to do in a car. Glancing back, I saw that Jack was still in second with his ridiculous painted car. I could sense his smugness, as he thought he was so good at racing, when really it was because he knew this city like the back of his hands.

That was cheating if you asked me.

After the hair pin turn, there was a large ramp that went up. I didn't remember this in the city before. I tried to remember during all my times on Recar. I guess I sort of remembered it, but wasn't it never…

Shit.

Cadi, be careful! Jack said, but it was too late, I couldn't avoid what came next.

The ramp was a dead-end, and we had to jump it to the next roadway. I screamed as my motorbike went flying through the air. Thank goodness I had a quick reaction and could use my powers to glide onto the roadway, instead of crashing and almost dying as I tumbled across the track with cars falling on top of me.

Well, that was a pleasant adrenaline rush.

Next time, at least, I would be prepared and could use my powers to get to the other side without having a panic attack. It was just this first time that it was iffy, but I managed. I released the breath I was holding and ventured to the next part of the track. I hoped it wasn't as frightening as that last part.

There were a lot of sharp turns on this track, which showed Kane how well these drivers could maneuver with their cars. I had no problem, as my motorcycle gave me a lot more control, so it wasn't hard to maintain my lead. Even Jack was having a bit of trouble with the turns.

The track still dumped out at the spot with the wave crashing over the side. I was able to dodge it this time without using my powers and kept propelling forward. Soon I was back at the start of the race.

Lap number two.

I could sense Jack on my tail, still trying to one-up me. We didn't say much during this round to each other, mainly because it took a lot of concentration to keep up with the turns and everything else. It was hard enough to just race and not crash, let alone focus on communicating through our connection.

My father also didn't try to talk to me, knowing this race was intense. I wondered where he was watching from, if it was from one of the buildings, on a screen, or if he was standing with the other people at the finish line, itching to see the victor. It wasn't like he had to worry about getting hurt if a car spun off at the finish line, as he could heal better than even I could.

I tried not to think about the crash that had happened when I raced the first time. It hadn't been my fault; those men were shooting at me. I had to protect myself. It was their fault, not my own.

It shouldn't have bothered me as much as it did. I had killed many people, including my own uncle, under duress of the Emperor's orders. It seemed different though, as it was an accident, and it was on my first mission. They were innocent people who just wanted to enjoy the races, even though accidents happened like that every time they held the tournament. I had to keep telling myself that.

I was coming up on the ramp, this time I was prepared for it. I let the air engulf me, as I focused on landing as delicately as I could. Hitting the ground, bracing myself for the slight sway of the vehicle, I kept forward and heard Jack hit the ground behind me. He was right on my tail now.

Glancing back, I found Alan, Logan, and Tim all right behind me as well. Tim's car kept crashing into Alan, and I could almost hear Alan's cussing as he tried to pass Tim. After a few moments, he was able to get around Tim and Logan's blockade, and enter third. Great, that meant the Republic might keep second and third. I had to make sure I would stay in first or else we might be screwed.

Then again, all I needed was second, not first.

Part of me just wanted to win all the races, as I had that competitive streak in me, and to prove to Jack motorbikes were better. I focused on the mission at hand, though, and didn't let that override why I was there: to collect the gem and get off of this planet.

That is if Kane didn't set up some blockade so I

couldn't leave. I knew once the races were over; I had to act quick. He didn't seem one who liked to be told no, let alone used for an extended amount of time. Then again, most people didn't.

Rounding the last corner before the crashing wave, I took a deep breath. I had a feeling this one would not be good. I could sense it—someone was going to use their powers, but I wasn't sure who. All I knew was I needed to brace myself.

The wave came crashing down on me and I felt the bike under me, not able to take it. It slid across the ground, turning. It took all of my strength not to roll and be taken out by the cars behind me. As I started to lose control, I aimed for the side of the road so Alan couldn't run over me.

With the water raining down on me, I wasn't able to keep the bike upright.

I slid across the ground into the side of the wall as cars sped past me. I took a deep breath as I stopped and regained my composure. I checked the bike quickly for damage and then raced forward before the two cars coming at me could pin me into the wall. Seconds later, one hit the side a little too hard, and their car was wrecked.

That's what he gets.

I was now in seventh place and would have to make it up on the last lap. The hard part wouldn't be gaining up on them, even with boosters, but making sure the cars didn't side swipe me.

Starting the final lap, I was able to get in front of two

cars with ease. They weren't the best racers, I could tell. Now I just had to get past the Imperial's and the Republic's cars, plus one from this planet.

Tim was the first car I needed to pass and even though he should let me get back to first, he was trying his best to stay in my way. Typical. He did, however, focus more on me than the pin turn and almost missed it.

I was able to pass him because of that mistake.

I watched as he slammed his hand into his steering wheel, his mouth making out words I presumed were cuss words. I laughed a little to myself. Served him right.

Next was the Recarian. He was too focused on the jump coming up to side swipe me. I passed him with ease right before I started up the ramp. I went off the edge away from where he was though, just in case he did accidently, or purposefully, land on me. I hit the ground without too much fuss and rode on after the last three cars.

Alan, who was in third now, did not want to let me pass and I could tell was thinking up a way to take me out. He wanted me dead more than my own brother did, although I didn't blame him. I had destroyed his life while I was the Emperor's Shadow. I was just doing what I had to do to survive. He should have understood, but he never did. He always tried to preach to me about morals and such, but I never listened. Morals were out the window for me a long time ago.

As I was just at his right taillight, he swerved to the right to clip me. Idiot should have known I predicted that, as I had slowed down just enough for him to miss me and then veered to the left and was able to pass him. I waved at him as I took third place.

Man, did he look pissed.

Now I just had two more people to pass. Jack was still in the lead with Logan right on his tail. Neither of them would, hopefully, try and take me out, or at least not on purpose. I could tell Logan was too focused on passing Jack to notice I was closing in on him.

We were coming up to the water. I wasn't looking forward to this, as I wasn't sure how the accident had happened last time. I felt it again, though, how a wave was coming from some sort of power. Then it occurred to me.

It was Logan. And this time he was trying to take out Jack.

Jack watch out!

I know. I can read minds, remember?

Right, he knew what was going through Logan's mind. He must have figured out who had done it last time and was keeping tabs on what he was doing to be sure. I watched as the giant wave came.

Jack might be able to dodge that, but I wasn't going to be able to.

I had to use my powers to block it, even if it would raise suspicion. I made a tunnel through the water for myself, also using my powers to go faster so no one would notice what had happened.

Making it through the other side, safe and sound, and also in first, I grinned. Yes, this was all going according to plan.

Cheater. Jack said in my mind.

Otherwise I would be in the sea right about now.

Fair, but now you are going to piss off all the racers. I would watch your back. Remember what happened last time?

I remembered. Some of the other racers tried to kidnap me, but I was able to take them out. That was why I always kept a gun and a couple of knives on me, except the other night which I regretted. I doubted it would happen this time, however, as the only people close in rank with me were Jack, Logan, Tim, and Alan. Unless they would take us all out, only a few of the others stood a chance.

But I would still be on alert. You never knew what crazy things people would do to win.

I passed the finish line, fireworks soaring in the air once again. I would need that mechanic again to clean up the scrapes from this race.

Chapter 10

Dennis was able to fix up my bike pretty quickly. I was quite impressed.

"I am surprised you didn't have more damage for when that wave hit you," he said as he wiped sweat off his brow. "I mean, if it were me, I would have totaled it."

"Yeah, well, that's because I'm a professional driver."

"I suppose so. I am surprised you didn't crash again with the second wave. How did you manage that?" he asked with such innocence.

I smiled. "It's because I was used to it by then. And I was able to outrun it before the major pressure hit me. It helped me get into the lead too, which I am thankful for."

"Yeah, I suppose so. There was a little water damage, however, with the engine. I was able to fix it up with no problem. It will ride as good as new tomorrow as well."

"Will? You sure sound full of yourself."

"I know I do good work, Miss Ryetirf. I assure you, I am the best you will find on this planet. Even Kane can vouch for me, which is not an easy recommendation to have."

I liked this kid. "No, I suppose it's not."

"Will you need anything else?"

I shook my head. "No, everything else is good. Go see what your mom is making you for dinner."

With that, he ran out of the garage like a little kid. For how good he was with machines, I forgot he was still younger than he appeared. I took another look at my bike. It looked as good as new. I thought it would have a lot more dents in it from how much I slid. He was one hell of a mechanic.

Locking up the garage, I headed back towards my hotel. It was almost dinner again, and I decided it would be best to have that risotto again, as it seemed to have brought me good luck so far. It knew it wasn't the food that caused me to win the races, but I had to convince myself it was to not feel bad about eating the same thing three days in a row.

As I headed back, I felt as if there was someone watching me. Again. I sighed. It was probably Jack being Jack—thinking I couldn't take care of myself. He was too overprotective sometimes, I swore.

Jack, I know it's you. I said with our connection.

What's me?

Don't play stupid, I don't have time.

No, seriously, Cadi, what is going on?

I turned around to find three sizable men gathered around me, one with a gun pointed straight at my head.

"Don't make a fuss and come with us," the man with the gun said.

Cadi? Talk to me…

Why did this always happen to me?

The men directed me towards some secluded garage on the north end of the city. I didn't want to make a scene on the streets and catch more attention since the journalists liked good gossip. If I shot these guys on the street, it would be all over the news and Kane would have a bigger mess to clean up. I mean, I didn't care about the last part, I more just didn't want to be on the news. Then I might have more people after me. I could take care of myself, but it was just such a hassle.

When we entered, the men forced me to sit on a wooden chair and tied me down with some rope. It would take little to no effort to get out of these, so I didn't resist. I wanted to see what they wanted at this point.

Glancing around at the inside of the garage, I found one of the cars I had passed near the end of the race. I think he ended up being fourth. Did he really think taking me out would give him a chance? I sighed. There were four other cars that I didn't recognize. Either they weren't in the races or they were so far back that they were idiotic to think they had any chance, unless some crazy shit happened, which, to be honest, did happen at times. I doubted the rankings would change much in this tournament, as there had never been Sanshlians racing before.

At least, not that I knew of.

Cadi, where are you? I can come get you.

No need, these guys are just a bunch of punks.

You said that last time and almost got killed by Damian.

No, you ran a car into his car and almost killed me.

But it was still his fault.

I tried not to roll my eyes and confuse the men that were holding me hostage. They didn't seem like the brightest, though, as they were still talking and arguing about what they would do with me. They weren't sure if they wanted to just scare me or actually kill me. I sighed. They needed to get their priorities straight.

A brown haired, blue eyed man about the height of Jack walked over to me, knife pulled out.

"Now, we are going to be very clear, we don't like hurting girls, but we need to win these races to pay off our debts."

Now I could roll my eyes. Of course they had debts. Who on this planet didn't? Having debts kept this planet's economy in motion.

"I don't care, you think this is the way you will win the races? With threats?"

They glanced at each other, then the main guy turned to me. "Yeah, we do."

I let out another sigh. "Look, I will give you guys one chance. If you want to make it out alive to see your families again, you should just let me go and try your best on the next round, okay?"

He laughed. "Are you threatening me? You are the one tied up and I am the one with the knife."

"I have traveled across the entire galaxy and have dealt with men like you everywhere I've gone. You aren't that hard to overpower."

His face was reddening. "Look, I am not joking, I will hurt you if I need to."

"I thought you said you don't like hurting girls."

"Just—Just withdraw from the races so I can win."

"You aren't even doing that well, there is at least three or four racers in front of you. What, are you going to dispose of all of them as well?"

"I… just shut up."

Why was it always so easy to get under the skin of men like this? I took in a deep breath and tested the strength of the ropes. Yeah, it would be easy to break out of these when the time came with my super strength.

"Look, I don't know if you actually think making me withdraw will help you out, or if you are just intimidated because a girl is beating you on a motorbike. Just put your masculine ego off to the side and train hard enough so you can beat me."

"That's it!" he lunged forward with the knife which was what I expected. I broke out of the rope and grab his wrist before he sliced open my stomach. The look of surprise on his face was priceless.

"Ah, ah. Didn't your mom teach you hurting girls is bad?" I smiled as I twisted his wrist. He screamed as the bones crunched in my grip. I snatched the knife up before it fell.

The other two men rushed forward to help their comrade out. I didn't know what they expected to do since neither of them reached for their guns yet. Typical.

As the first one who had blond hair and was quite tall charged forward, I dug the knife straight into his side. I heard a rib crunch. Thank goodness for super strength, otherwise fighting these guys would have taken a lot longer. The man screamed in pain as I yanked it out, blood dripping down the knife. He went down, holding his side, cussing at me.

"You bitch! What the hell?!"

The third man tried to rush me from behind and I flipped the knife around and drove it into his stomach. He was short, stout, and had jet black hair. Blood came pouring out of his mouth as he collapsed to the ground. I doubted he would recover from that, even if his friends took him straight to the hospital.

"Now, now, what to do with bad boys such as yourselves..." I tapped the knife on the side of the chair. "Should I let my attackers live or should I put some dogs out of their misery?"

The main guy pulled out his gun with his good hand and pointed it at me, his face redder than an apple. "Bitch, you will die for that!"

Before he could shoot, I ran forward and drove the knife straight into his throat. Blood splashed across the area, soiling my shirt and pants. I always hated that part —death was always messy, or at least when I was involved. He dropped the gun as his body collapsed to the floor, a pool of blood forming around him.

The man with the rib injury reached for his gun as I bent down and grabbed the one that was on the ground. Within an instant, I shot him in the head before he could even react. The other man was still gurgling blood. I shot him in the head to put him out of his misery.

Guess they didn't want to survive this. Weirdly, the people who decided to kidnap me always chose this route. I never understood that, as I always gave them the option to run.

I examined the gun and decided to keep it. It was a rather nice-looking gun, and I could always use an extra. Looting the main guy's body, I found my own gun and two knives they had taken off of me on the street.

Debating on letting Kane know what happened, I decided to get an IK to tell him for me. It seemed only decent, and it would save him time from putting in an investigation of where these men disappeared to. He and I already agreed that if I was ever attacked, I could use any means to keep myself safe. These men weren't Imperial or Republic, but I felt that the offer included other racers as well, especially ones as dirty as these three.

I left the garage and found three kids that looked like they could take information to Kane for me. I told them to tell Kane that some clean-up was needed at the garage. I wrote the address and gave the kids a few coins. They hurried off toward his office. I may have paid them a little too much, but that was okay. At least I knew they would have a few meals in the coming days.

All is good, Jack. Took care of the idiots.

You have the best of luck, Cadi, I swear.
Yeah, well, you know me.

Chapter 11

I was quick to enter the hotel with no one noticing my clothes were covered in blood and went straight to my room to rinse off and change. I threw the dirty clothes in the trash, not worried that the cleaners here would say anything as it wasn't out of the norm to find blood-ridden clothes in the trash. There were a lot of brawls in this city.

After I stepped out of the shower, I saw that it was already late. I hoped that the restaurant was still open, though I had a feeling it would be on this planet. I ordered another plate of risotto and watched a replay of the races as I waited for room service to bring me my food.

I wanted to make sure no one could tell what had happened on the last lap with the wave, or at least that it didn't look too strange. When the replay got to that part, the camera angle made it impossible to tell what happened, and it appeared I had just missed the wave.

Thank goodness.

There was a soft knock at my door, and something told me it wasn't room service. I grabbed my gun and peaked through the peephole. I barely made out a young girl standing at the door. I opened up.

She said nothing, but handed me a note and ran off. I closed the door and opened up the letter.

Thanks. ~Kane

Really, did he need to send me this note? I guess he just wanted to let me know he got the information. I tossed it on the counter and collapsed on the bed.

Ugh, why did these things always happen to me?

The next knock on my door was my meal, and I gobbled it up in a flash. I was hungry before those men so rudely kidnapped me and made me kill them, not to mention using my super strength left me pretty hungry. With a full belly, I decided I should let Nygard know what Logan did, even though I knew Logan would give me crap for tattling on him. It wasn't my fault he almost caused me to lose my bike.

Father, did you notice the powers used during the race?

It took him a moment to respond. *Yes, and it already has been dealt with.*

He wasn't aiming for me, but Jack.

It doesn't matter; he put you in jeopardy, and at this point you are the only chance we have at winning first.

I debated on telling him at this point that we just

needed second place, but I didn't want to piss him off since he seemed angry already. I couldn't blame him.,.

I thought you said never to presume the future until it is the present, or something like that.

You know what I mean. These races aren't safe, and it seems like every car wants to take you out. I don't need my own men doing the same.

It was best not to tell him about the three men who had just kidnapped me. *The person I am worried most about taking me out is Alan. I think he might not like me.*

Don't worry about him, his rage is too strong for him to think clearly. He won't have a chance beating you.

I felt a little secure hearing him say that, but I knew better than that. Alan was a force to be reckoned with, that was a fact. He would risk everything to take me out. *I won't let worry cloud my judgment, father, but I still want to be cautious. We have a lot to lose.*

You will do fine, I believe in you. Now get some rest, it is getting late. I have a feeling the race tomorrow will be even more difficult.

I knew he was right. I let the connection disconnect and let the physical exhaustion my mind was apparently ignoring consume me.

Giant trees surrounded me as I pushed my way past the foliage that made up this jungle. This place felt so familiar, as if I had been here before. I tried to remember the name as it was on the tip of my tongue, but I couldn't remember.

I couldn't remember anything.

All I knew was I had to move forward, as if something was calling me in the distance. It was like hearing a siren's call and I was caught up in its trance.

"*Kibs yh, sbiohi hoji yh,*" the voice called out.

Branches scratched my arms and legs that were not covered in cloth, and snagged at my tank-top and shorts, but I did not care. All I knew was that I needed to keep moving forward.

Even though the song was beckoning me, I did not move at a faster pace. I was almost in a daze—simply moving at a relaxed speed, but no matter how hard I tried, I could not stop. I took in the space around me, smelling the citrus scent of the trees, the sweetness of the white flowers that covered many of the bushes, and the earthy smell that was brought up from the ground as I walked. If I didn't know better, this place would seem like paradise.

Yet, somewhere in my mind, I knew this wasn't paradise—this was a place where a lot of pain and suffering had happened.

The air was thick with the energy of something violent that had happened. It felt as if a thousand ghosts were haunting this area. Why couldn't I remember where I was? Why couldn't I remember what had happened here?

Why did my mind feel like it was a giant blank?

I stepped through an opening in the forest, and before me was a giant waterfall. The air was warm and humid, small droplets of water hitting my skin, soothing the scratches the planets had caused.

Suddenly I felt it: a giant rush of energy passing through me. I gasped, trying to understand what was going on. The singing was louder now, almost as if it was coming from every direction.

"*KIBS YH, SBIOHI HOJI YH!*"

Darkness came soaring out of the water, its tendrils going every which way like a giant octopus. I watched as everywhere the tendrils touched turned into death. The energy of every living thing was being sucked out in an instant. Everything was being absorbed by whatever creature this was. Fear filled my entire body, and I didn't know what to do.

Was there anything I could even do?

The tendrils swung every which way, destroying the entire forest around me, each one missing me by an inch. Even though they never touched me, I could still feel the evil energy that they released. It felt like a thousand needles being stabbed into my skin and into my bones. This was something I never wanted to feel again—this was something that shouldn't exist.

The entire planet was destroyed now. The only living thing left was me and this creature that lay before me. I stared up at it, not sure why it hadn't harmed me.

And that was when I saw it—a man floating above the monster.

"Father?"

I jumped up out of bed, taking a deep breath. My pajamas were soaked from sweat. I stood there, staring at my bed, not sure what I had just witnessed. I used to have dreams of Sanshli before we found the planet, and about when we found the planet, but I had never had a dream like that before.

What was that creature? And why did I just dream about it now?

The dream had felt so real. Were the spirits of the planet trying to warn me about my father? Did he have a creature like that, or was it just a symbolism of the destruction he had caused?

Taking a deep breath, I lay back down on the bed. It was just a dream, or at least that was what I kept telling myself. It couldn't hurt me. It wouldn't hurt me.

Unless that was a warning of what would happen if I betrayed Nygard.

Chapter 12

It was the third day of the races. I sat in my first-place mark, waiting for the race to start. I was still shaken-up from the dream I had, although I did fall back asleep and dreamed of nothing in particular. At least there was that.

The rain was a slight drizzle, which was better than the night before when it was pouring. It was the only problem I had about being on the motorbike: rain, or just water in general.

I wondered what extra goodies this day of the race would have. The third race was when things like people shooting at you, obstacles, or a mix of both was introduced into the race. I couldn't wait to see what happened while I was on the bike. At least this jumpsuit and helmet was bulletproofed.

Or at least I hoped it was. I would find out the truth

soon.

I also had a feeling if there was gunfire, they would really go after me as it didn't seem that anyone liked me too much since I was both a girl and not driving a car. Most of the winners throughout history were men, not because women weren't good, but because they weren't stupid enough to put their life on the line for something like this.

Yeah, I admit, I was pretty stupid. But I liked the adrenaline rush.

Hey, how was last night? Jack asked. I swore he was just trying to distract me so he could get a leg up, or he just missed me that much.

Which part? The kidnapping or the nightmares?

Both, I guess?

Well, you saw what happened with the guys, as they were taken out of the race line up. The nightmares… are worse than the ones I had before we were on Sanshli.

Really? What were they about?

Just Sanshli stuff. I don't want to talk about it right now.

Well maybe later tonight then?

We will see. I didn't want him to think he could come over. It would make him just a little too cocky.

The light blinked and the crew, once again, got off of the track. I watched as the light blinked its last red light and revved my engine in anticipation.

The light turned green.

I launched forward, getting a head start as my bike accelerated faster than the cars. I debated letting Jack go ahead of me so he would shield me from any obstacles, but then Alan would be close enough to me to take me out. I wasn't sure which was more dangerous.

Probably the obstacles.

As Jack came up to my speed, I let him pass me. I knew he was sporting a cocky grin as he passed me, thinking he had outdone me. He should have known better.

As if on cue, a rain of bullets hit Jack's car, and I ducked, using his car as my shield.

Oh, you she-devil.

You should know this race well enough to realize that was coming.

Yeah, yeah, I let you use me as a shield.

Sure.

They must have had automatic rifles as the bullets kept pouring. How did they expect anyone to drive through this? I stayed behind Jack's car, glancing over to make sure he was fine. He was, as the bullets had hit the back door of his car. He must have upgraded to a bulletproof car, as it didn't seem like the bullets were going through anything.

Bulletproof car?

Of course. I don't want to die in these races, it would be a waste of my good looks.

Right…

The gunmen stopped aiming at us and went down the line. I sighed as I bent back up, letting Jack take the lead once again. I had a feeling that wasn't the only thing I had to watch out for.

There weren't as many hair pin turns as there were last

time, but there were still quite a bit of turns, not to mention this lap felt a lot longer than any previous race. Maybe I was wrong and there were no other obstacles. It was just the length of this lap.

And I had spoken too soon.

We were at a dead-end. Shit. I did not see this coming. This meant that we would have to turn around and do the lap backwards.

With other cars coming at us at the same time.

At least the dead-end was a roundabout and it would be a little easier to turn around for the cars. I didn't have any problem turning around. I just had to worry that someone would come straight at me.

Like Alan for example.

I could dodge him this time, but I knew he would try that again, not to mention the half a dozen racers behind him that wanted to do the same thing to me.

See, my kidnappers should have just waited until this race. They could have had a better chance at taking me out.

Or at least my bike, as I would only get injured by getting hit by any of these cars. Most would die, but I would just suffer for a bit before getting healed, as long as someone didn't destroy anything vital such as irreversible damage to either my heart or brain. I wasn't sure how that would happen, but I knew it would kill me. It was one of the few ways I could die.

Swerving through the remaining cars, I was able to miraculously not get hit, as a lot of them tried to aim for me. Jack still had the lead, and I let him keep it, hiding behind him so I wouldn't get hit by the other cars, or the guns. As long as I stayed behind him, survived, and got second place, all I had to do was get third in the next round.   This was my best bet at getting through this round, and not like I was doing it on purpose.

We were coming up to where the men shooting at the contestants were located. I was going to hate this part, especially since it would happen twice with each lap. Letting out a sigh, I ducked to the side of Jack's car.

Then the rain of bullets began.

And, apparently, I wasn't ducking well enough this time, or some men got in a better position to take me out. Three bullets embedded into my jumpsuit. Although it was bulletproofed, and the cloth was able to stop them, that didn't mean it didn't hurt.

Damn it to the far reaches of the galaxy…

You okay? Both Nygard and Jack asked. I had never had them both try to talk to me at the same time; it was rather weird.

Yeah, I'm fine. I thought back to both of them. In a few moments, the area would heal and I wouldn't feel the pain anymore, but the initial impact always hurt.

The bullets stopped hitting the side of Jack's car and I backed away a little. I wasn't sure how the turnaround at the start of the race would work and I figured Jack would be a good person to go first again to figure it out. If I wasn't mistaken, there was a roundabout right behind where we started and I just didn't notice.

I glanced behind me to find Logan and Alan right on my tail. Great, if there was a turnaround, they would be close enough to possibly try to take me out. Logan shouldn't be aiming to hit me, but if Alan provoked him, he might come crashing into me. And Alan, well, he was always aiming for me.

With a deep sigh, I focused on what was in front of me: Jack and the next roundabout.

The crowd at the finish line cheered as we came dangerously close to them. The roundabout spelled disaster for this area, did they not realize that? This would be where everyone might collide and yet they stood there, acting like everything was fine and dandy. Such idiotic people. I guess that was what made it all fun: the possibility that all these colliding cars could burst into flames.

Jack's wheels screeched as he took the turn as fast as he could. Even I felt a little wary of how fast he was taking it. But that was Jack for you. He was always willing to take the risk to come out as the winner. That was what I loved about him.

And that was what he loved about me.

I knew if I slowed down, I was screwed, so I took the turn on the bike as fast as I could without flipping. It was close. If I took it only a tiny bit faster, I would be flung off the bike. I may or may not have used my powers a little to make sure I didn't lose complete control.

But I succeeded.

Now I just had to dodge the cars coming at me once again. Staying right on Jack's tail made it a lot easier, as the cars didn't want to go head on with another car.

Lucky me.

Jack was making it easy for me to stay close to him, which probably looked weird to all the other drivers and anyone who was watching. Normally everyone wanted to take each other out, but we acted like a team which would probably bring up more questions from Kane, not that I really cared. I just had to finish the race tomorrow, get the trophy, and get out of here.

But as I always knew, nothing ever went according to plan.

I just hoped that we would all survive this and could go home, wherever that was. I didn't know what timeline was really my home anymore, nor even what planet. If Sanshli was like the dream I had, I didn't want to go back, nor would I feel like it was my home. Or maybe it was, and the dream was about me destroying any chance I had at home.

I didn't know anymore.

Jack was doing good on this day of the race. I wondered if it was because it was more his style: guns pointed at him and cars coming every which way. I mean, he definitely had been in quite a few shootouts, and chases through this city and the neighboring city of Nyct. And I mean, a lot. Heck, I think there had been at least half a dozen of them.

Which is what made me worry whenever I wasn't on the planet.

Don't get me wrong, I believed Jack could get out of a scrape he was in, but there were constantly people after him and that scared me at times. Then again, he worried about me as I had a whole galaxy of people who wanted me dead. I guess we both liked it that way to an extent. It did make life more interesting, to say the least.

I was able to dodge the gunmen this time around. They had three more chances to take me out. I hoped I wasn't getting too cocky about it. Knowing my luck, they would get in a position to take me out.

The turnaround was as easy as it would ever get. This time, two cars crashed head on, leaving a fiery explosion in my mirror. I hoped they would clear it out before we came back around, or it would cause even more crashes.

Then again, I felt like they might keep it there as a bonus obstacle.

As we came upon the shooters, I noticed that they got into better positions. It would be near impossible for them to miss me.

Well shit.

At least five, maybe six or seven, bullets hit me straight in my chest, the impact made me almost lose my balance. I would have if I didn't have my Sanshlian powers.

I breathed into them, focusing on healing. It would take a few moments, and the next turn would be very, very uncomfortable as I waited for any of those superficial impacts to heal.

Now I would have to watch them once again in the next go around.

I decided it would be best to pass Jack on the roundabout so I could quickly weave through the gunfire on the last lap. I would take the lead in the beginning and all the way through, then with the last shower of bullets, I would act a little hurt and he could pass me.

Yeah, that sounded like a good plan.

I weaved through the oncoming cars and headed straight towards the fun area at full speed. This would be my only chance at getting through without getting shot.

Or I would get riddled with bullets. It honestly could go either way.

I weaved back and forth, trying to take a haphazard route so they couldn't predict where I was going. Even I wasn't sure which way I would turn as it was all happening so fast.

Only one bullet hit me. Barely. It grazed the cloth of my arm. Thank goodness, now I could finish healing the last wounds and get on with this race.

And tomorrow's race would be even harder. Great.

I forgot how long this course was until the turn around. Without Jack ahead of me, it felt like it was all just open road. I didn't know if I liked it better or worse. I liked the solitude that came with being in a distant first, with everything behind me, but I also liked the feeling of security that Jack gave me.

I guessed he was right behind me, so I didn't need to feel alone.

They cleared off the racetrack before we made it back to where the two cars had collided. I was rather surprised, as I would have thought it would have made a great obstacle, although it obstructed a good chunk of the area, making it impossible for two cars to pass each other, and there would have been even more crashes.

Whatever, I was on a motorbike and would have been able to weave my way around it.

I made my way through the cars coming at me and noted who was right behind me. Jack was on my tail, as usual, while Alan and Logan were still right behind him. My plan would still work as we went through the area with the gunmen. Perfect.

The gunmen aimed straight at me, not letting up. I slowed down just a tad so Jack could take the lead and I hid right behind him, only getting a couple shots straight in the arm.

Just endure it, I told myself. You only need to do this one last time.

And that was when I saw a piece of metal come exploding out of the ground and straight into the side of my wheel.

"Son of a—"

Chapter 13

I was glad I had a lot better control of my powers now. The moment I noticed the metal going into my bike wheel, I slowed time enough that I could perform a miraculous jump towards the car behind me, which was Alan's. I didn't care if my landing would dent his car, because running over my bike would definitely do some damage to his car, anyway.

Screw him.

He was ready to run me over. I knew he wanted to, but to actually try was a whole different story. He would pay later, I swore. If my father didn't take him out when all of this was over, I most definitely was going to.

I shook the thought out of my head. No, I wasn't my father. I wouldn't kill him just because he was a fool. I would learn from my father's mistakes and become better than him—better than I used to be.

It was hard to believe that when I took out all those guys last night.

But they were going to kill me. I had to do it.

The fact that I was starting to have a conscience was weirding me out. But I needed to focus on the task at hand.

I hit Alan's car with a loud thud and time went back to normal. I held on to the front of his hood for dear life because I knew he would try his hardest to throw me off. To my surprise he didn't slow down, knowing full well it could cost him the race. I held on, anticipating what he would do next, and debated what I should do to stay in the top three.

Cadi!

Yeah, I know. Do me a favor and read Alan's mind and let me know when he will try to turn to get me off of his hood.

Will do. We don't have much farther so you will have to react fast.

Clearly, I can.

I took in what was going on around me. Alan was in second place with Jack in first. Behind Alan was Logan hot on his tail. We were coming to the very end of the track and it was only a matter of time before I either needed to hold on or trying something very, very stupid to beat Alan.

But I forgot one thing. We were still in the area for the gunmen.

Bullets rained across Alan's hood and I let out a shout in pain. At least a dozen bullets embedded themselves into my jumpsuit across my back, leaving bruises and a couple of broken bones.

"Damn it!"

I would heal, I kept telling myself. Just beat Alan and piss him off.

The bullets hitting me must have distracted Alan as Logan was able to get around him and get to second place. There was still some stretch to go, but the odds were Alan wouldn't make that up. I had to beat Alan now to keep my guaranteed second place.

"Son of a bitch!" I could hear Alan in the car. He was not happy about Logan passing him, but that was what he got for the stunt he pulled. Plus, he would be even more pissed when he saw what I was going to do.

We were only a few hundred meters from the finish line and was able to pull myself up into a kneeled position, hoping I could pull off what I wanted to do without getting run over.

The only problem was, Alan knew exactly what I was going to do, which would throw him in fourth place. Luckily, I had an ace up my sleeve.

Cadi, he is going to spin the car right, so jump to your left!

I was able to turn just as Alan swerved right, spinning the car attempting to prevent me from jumping forward and reaching the finish line before him. Unfortunately for him, he didn't know I had a way of finding out which way he would turn. If he was going to use his power to control metal, I was going to use mine in the way I saw fit.

Just to make sure I didn't screw up, I slowed down

time so I could get a better understanding where I needed to land so I didn't get run over. It didn't seem like a pleasant experience, and if I could, I wanted to avoid it at all costs. If I got the right momentum, I could jump at an angle where I would make the corner of the finish line and make my way to the barricades towards the audience. I had no idea what they would do to me if I ran over and jumped the barricades, but it would be better than getting caught on the racetrack without a vehicle.

Hopefully luck was on my side.

I figured out what angle I need to jump at and at what time I needed to jump and time started up again. I leaped off of the car just as I planned, getting across the finish line before Alan. That asshole deserved to be screwed over like this and I hoped I would be able to see his face after all this was over. Also, I wanted to go after him and punch him in the nose, but didn't need the video all over the city. I would deal with him later, though, that was for damn sure. But at the moment, I needed to focus on rolling towards the barricades, and audience, and getting up to the finish line before someone swerved in my direction.

Hitting the ground hurt as much as I thought it would, if not more. Any normal person would have broken a few bones, and to be honest I think I did too except in my case I could heal them in an instant, even faster now that father taught me how to. There was no wonder why people thought he was invincible. I almost felt like I was too. I was happy I was wearing a helmet though.

Also, the pain might not have seemed as bad since I had taken so many bullets in the past hour.

I rolled across the street and got up as quickly as I could and jumped on the other side of the barricades. These drivers may be dicks, but they wouldn't risk innocent lives to get to me, or at least I hoped.

"We can't believe it! Arcadia has come in at third place! What a miracle! I have never seen anything like it!" The announcer screamed through the speakers. Flashes of light surrounded me as everyone took my picture—a picture of the girl who defied all odds.

They had no idea.

I took my helmet off and hurried over towards where the cars were lining up to see what the head of the races had to say for herself. Just because I made it across the line didn't mean I could still qualify. My bike was in shambles now and I doubted that I could get it fixed, even with the miraculous Dennis fixing it. It had been my favorite one too, as it rode so smoothly. I wasn't sure what I would do now without raising suspicion from Kane. That was for later though, as I needed to hear what was going on next.

The rest of the remaining cars came in and the street was finally safe. I knew Jack was probably terrified and ready to kill Alan. He couldn't do anything without Kane noticing, so I knew he would wait. As for me punching Alan, that would have to happen later. Hopefully I could do just that within the next few hours though, as I had a lot of rage ready to be unleashed.

"First place goes to Xander Vanguard!" The crowd roared for Jack, as his name in this life was Xander.

"Second place goes to Peter Haas!" More cheering. They didn't even know who he was, and they cheered anyway. It was strange.

"Third place, even without her bike, is Myra Ryetirf!"

So they did still keep my ranking. Thank goodness, otherwise I would have had to tell Tim and Logan that I had been lying and the crystal was in fact in the second-place trophy, or steal the trophy from whoever won.

I ran towards where my bike was pushed to the side of the racetrack against the barriers. It was in three pieces and bent into a shape it was never designed for, and totally not repairable.

"Son of a bitch," I whispered as I threw the piece I had in my hand to the ground. "I'm going to kill him."

A couple of the crew came over to, what I presume, examine me, but I pushed past them without a word. I needed to get out of here and get some fresh air.

And then punch someone's face in.

Chapter 14

I walked straight through Himeo, with no proper direction in mind, just wanting to walk off the anger. It wouldn't be enough to get all of my rage out, but it would be enough for me not to set the entire city on fire.

After the initial adrenaline from the race wore off, I was even more angry at Alan and the shit he pulled. I should have just used my own power to destroy his car and show him what it was like. There was nothing stopping me from doing it now, but I felt like it would be poor sportsmanship, and all that shit.

But I would go and punch him later. First, I had to let off a little more steam, or I might actually kill him.

But would that really be so bad?

I didn't know why I hadn't done it yet—killed him and saved myself all this trouble. I was under the same roof as him for an entire year and did nothing but play their stupid games. I could have taken them all out if I wanted, but for some reason I didn't.

Maybe it was because I killed their father. I had killed my uncle.

Why this fact was eating at me was even more irritating than what had just happened on the racetrack. Did this have anything to do with the dream last night? Or the fact my father had destroyed everything in his path no matter who it was, just like I had when I was the Emperor's Shadow? Was I a monster just like him?

I needed a drink.

Turning to the closest bar, I entered to find it quite empty for Recar. I didn't care; it was better this way. I took a seat at the end of the bar and waved to the waiter.

"What will it be?" He asked me as he cleaned one of the glasses.

"The house whiskey. Straight."

The man nodded and poured the mixed whiskey into a glass and slid it to me. I downed it in one gulp.

"Another."

He gave me a look but said nothing as he poured more into the glass. This time I didn't down it but sipped on it, letting the initial shot start to warm up my body, and calm my nerves.

And boy, did I need it.

"Haven't seen many women like you down whiskey so fast. I am impressed."

I turned to find a woman sitting next to me. She had curly black hair that went down to her shoulders, a red dress that was rather tight on her body, with high heels and lipstick to match. I gave her a shrug.

"Long day."

The woman gave a half grin. "I bet."

"Look, I don't want to make small talk right now. I just want to finish this drink and calm my ass down. Then go beat up an asshole."

"You mean the guy who almost ran you over?" she asked.

I almost choked on the whiskey. I didn't know why her recognizing me was such a surprise, but it had caught me off guard.

She laughed. "Relax, I'm not going to go get the press or anything. I just came over here to tell you a lot of us are glad you are in the races. In a motorbike, nonetheless."

I gave her a perplexed look. "What do you mean?"

"Look, it's not often that a woman is able to get into the races, let alone be in the top three. There are many reasons for that, mainly because all the men here are pig. Those who do get in mean a lot to us girls who aren't able to get out of our positions. We just do what we can to survive."

I knew the feeling.

I looked down at my glass and swirled the contents. "I didn't realize."

"I had a feeling you didn't, that's why I came over here and tell ya. Thank you."

I turned back to face her, shaking my head. "You shouldn't be thanking me. I'm here for different reasons than that, none of which are worthy of your thanks."

"It doesn't matter. You are still an icon and will make girls have someone to look up to."

That was a strange thought, but I knew I wasn't worthy of such things. "They need better role models on this planet then."

She laughed. "Yeah, I agree. But you will do."

I took another sip. "Thanks for coming over here, I needed the distraction."

"No problem. Seemed like it was a crazy track. I'm surprised you aren't in the hospital."

"What do you think the whiskey is for?" I said. She had a point, I should have been in a hospital.

"Do you know the guy in the car that got first place? Throughout most of the race he seemed to not mind you next to him. Most racers would have sideswiped you if you were that close."

I examined her for a moment, wondering if she was lying about helping the press. It wasn't like I would give her the details of the relationship between the two of us either way, but that question seemed oddly specific.

Then again, I would have asked the same thing if I were on this planet.

"I have crossed paths with him before. He has good sportsmanship, and I knew he wouldn't take me out."

She nodded. "That's what I thought."

I wondered if she was just saying that or not. I downed the rest of my drink and placed some money on the table. "I better head out. It was nice to meet you…" I realized I had never asked her name.

She held out her hand. "Michelle."

I shook her hand. "Nice to meet you, Michelle."

"Wait just a second." She reached in her bag and handed me a card. "If you need anything, just call. I am always happy to help out a fellow woman."

She was a call girl. I smiled. "Thank you. Now, I've got to go punch a man's face in."

"You show him what a girl is capable of!"

Chapter 15

With my powers, I was able to sense where my brother was. And where my brother was, Alan would be as well.

They had an apartment somewhere on the south side of the city. The closer I got, the stronger I could feel them. I didn't think I would need to go find them, which was why I never asked where they were staying. I was supposed to keep my distance from the Republic driver, but I couldn't resist getting my revenge.

I'm sure Kane would understand.

I just hoped that Jack wouldn't be there, waiting to stop me from making what he might call "a mistake". It wouldn't be a mistake, but more of what I called "a necessity". That is, if Jack hadn't already taken a swing or two at him. He was better at keeping his cool, but not when it came to me.

It was about a fifteen-minute walk from the bar I had just left, which wasn't too bad. Surprisingly enough, no one had stopped me in the streets. I guess people didn't look up at who was around them. I thought maybe people would realize I was a racer since I was still in my jumpsuit with bullets embedded throughout it.

I made a mental note to go grab another one on my way back to my hotel room. That is, if I needed one. I still didn't have a car and wasn't sure what I would do next. Nygard had resources he could use to get me another bike. I shouldn't worry, but I couldn't help it.

To think of it, it surprised me he hadn't tried to communicate with me. Maybe he just figured I needed some space or was mad that I had used my powers for the entire world to see. Or a little bit of both.

That would be future me's problem. Right now, I had to focus on the problem in front of me, which was a door.

I kicked the door in front of me open that led into the small apartment that my brother and his colleagues were staying in. The first person who's eyes I met were my brother's, and he didn't even react to me kicking their door down.

"Oh, sister, I expected you to come around, eventually."

I could feel raw energy radiating off my skin. I tried to take deep breaths, but I was far past being able to calm myself down. I had hoped the whiskey would do something, but I was wrong. "And you know damn well why. One of your men tried to kill me!"

Wesley let out a small sign. "Calm down, you know as

well as I that you wouldn't have died."

"But then all of Recar would have known I could heal myself, and that would just bring on a bunch of other problems that we do not need to deal with right now."

"Like that didn't already happen. You got shot multiple times and hit the ground hard, yet could somehow just get up and walk it off. You think people don't already suspect something is up?"

"It wouldn't have been so bad if Alan didn't try to kill me!"

He didn't even get up from his desk. "Not my problem."

I could kill him—I could kill him right then and there, and I wouldn't have to deal with his bullshit any longer. However, I knew our father, the father that had raised us both, would haunt me for the rest of eternity if I did such a thing.

Not that he didn't already haunt me, along with our uncle.

Lance Greel, once David Basen and the one person who I could tolerate, cleared his throat. I didn't even notice he was in the room. I snapped my gaze towards him, giving him a look to speak up. "Arcadia, think before you act."

I narrowed my eyes at him. "Tell that to your friends."

"He didn't mean to—"

I held up my hand. "Don't even finish that sentence, Lance, or I swear I will shoot you right here and now."

"Sister…"

"Don't sister me! You don't have any right to call me

your sister when you would be happy if Alan was successful in killing me! You lost the right to call me sister when you kidnapped me on Anosira to start this stupid quest!"

Wesley stood up and walked over to face me, his eyes inches from my own. "And you lost the right to call me brother when you joined the Empire and killed our uncle. Then you killed my wife."

I growled. "I didn't kill your wife, that was Tom."

"But it was your fault."

"I didn't want her to die, and you know that."

His face turned red as he started shouting. "Do I? Do I know that when you have killed so many of the PAE? So many innocent people have died at your hand that I bet you have lost count at this point!"

He paused, as if waiting for me to answer that. I didn't answer because he was right. I had lost count so long ago.

"Yeah, that was what I thought." He turned and went back to his seat.

"You have no idea what I have gone through." My voice wavered, and I could almost feel tears coming up. I didn't know what they were for—the people I had killed, the life I had led, or the fact my own brother thought I was a monster.

"And you have no idea what went on in my life after that night. I just didn't turn my back on our father's wishes."

"I never had the luxury of that choice."

"You could have said no."

"Then I would have died."

"And a lot fewer people would have suffered if you had."

His words hurt. His words hit hard. Lance looked like he would step forward and try to comfort me, but I gave him a look that said if he came anywhere near me, I would punch him in the stomach.

But at least someone cared.

I heard someone step up behind me. I turned around and the moment I saw it was Alan, I remembered why I was here. Now I had a lot more rage pent up inside. He couldn't even react fast enough as I punched him square in the nose. He went straight down to his knees, blood pouring all over the ground. I must have broken it good.

Alan looked up at me, eyes starting to water from the pain. "You bitch!"

"Bitch?!" I yelled down at him. "You were the one who was ready to run me over you piece of shit! Now I have to find a new ride!"

"Good! There was no way we would have let you win! That saved us the ordeal of having to come after you tonight."

I laughed. "I would have liked to see you try. Then you would have ended up like the men who tried to threaten me last night."

Alan got up and tried to punch me, but I caught his arm. He tried to switch arms and punch with his left, but I grabbed that one too and flung him over my shoulder. His back hit the ground hard. I doubted the impact broke any bones though, which was a shame.

He didn't get back up, but bent forward onto his elbows. Lance went down to check up on him. I was surprised Alan didn't make him go away.

Alan looked up at me. "There is no way in hell we will let you win, Arcadia! You know that, right? I mean, we can't trust you, not after what happened on Sanshli!"

I couldn't believe what I was hearing. After everything that had happened on Sanshli, these people should have been trusting me more. "You mean when you guys didn't care that I stood up and tried to kill the Emperor for you and he opened up my mind to a million spirits which all tried to speak to me all at once and I almost went insane?" I asked. "But yeah, don't trust me."

"Then why are you with them now? Why do you insist on always being on their side?"

It was a lot more complicated than a quick argument-scream match could explain. "Maybe because I have a little more freedom and I can direct them the way I want to. Or maybe because they don't treat me like trash like the lot of you do!"

"Or is it because your real father is with them, and you could finally follow straight into his footsteps!" Alan went on. "Something you didn't think of telling any of us!"

I couldn't believe what I was hearing. Did Jack tell them about Nygard?

Suddenly I felt another person walk into the room and all four of us raised our guns. It was Jack.

"Cadi! What happened? Are you okay?"

I didn't answer, but turned towards the door I had

busted to leave. Jack grabbed my wrist.

"Let. Me. Go." I growled. His eyes narrowed.

"What is going on?"

"I don't want to talk to you right now. I am pissed."

Then talk to me like this.

I said I don't want to.

Why are you here? *What about Kane's men?*

A little late for that now, don't you think? I mean, I had to break Alan's nose or I just wouldn't have been satisfied.

But why are you pissed?

Because you told them about Nygard.

He hesitated enough that I slipped out of his grip and head down the street. He ran after me.

"Cadi, wait!"

"I said no!"

He didn't seem to care as he chased me down the street. I debated giving up and just facing him, and not acting like a little kid, but I was furious, and I didn't want to do anything to Jack that I might have regretted.

Like shooting him in the head, or something.

Finally, when I felt that I had calmed down enough, I turned down an alleyway and stopped.

"Let me explain."

I gestured around. "No one is here, so get to explaining."

He leaned against the wall with his hand. "Give me a sec, I am out of breath."

"Liar, tell me right now, or so help me Jack…"

He sighed. "Fine, give me a sec to find the right words." He paused a moment and closed his eyes. I waited, rather impatiently of course.

"Second is up, Jack."

"I had to tell them because they wouldn't come to the races otherwise. Telling them about the gem wasn't enough. They figured that we wouldn't be able to do anything with it and decided that they would just interfere after the races were over, but I knew that wouldn't be good enough. So I told them Nygard was here so they would all come."

I let the words sink in and tried to soften my anger. It was working a little. I understood why he did it, but I wasn't sure I could forgive him for not running it by me first.

"As long as you or I win, we will get the gem and we will make them all go to Sanshli with us, right?"

I nodded slowly. "Yeah. As long as I don't kill my brother first."

"Cadi.."

"I know we need all of them to revert time back to how it was, but do you think if I just kill my brother and his friends, and then take their dead bodies with me we'd still be able to return to our proper time? Because I feel like it's a chance I should take."

"Cadi…"

"I know, I know, but the old me would have done it without hesitation. I feel I'm going soft and need to kill something to prove that I'm wrong."

Jack laughed. "I don't know, those moves you showed on the track were very Cadi-like. I would say you have everything still under control, if not better at it."

"Yeah, Nygard taught me a lot these past few months."

Jack was silent for a moment, as if trying to find the right words to ask me about Nygard. I could feel him judging me—as if getting close to my actual father was wrong.

"Do you think his power is a good idea? I mean, it was what caused all this in the first place."

"Only because everyone turned on him. I mean, if I look at my own past and all the things I've done, I can't blame him, now can I?"

"Cadi…"

"Seriously, Jack, how many people do you think I've killed over the years? And if I had his power, if I had gone through his torture, would I have not done the same?"

"He killed his own people."

"I killed my own uncle."

Jack was silent. I had told him the story a long time ago, confessing what I did to someone. He knew, under the circumstances, he would have done the same. So why was Nygard any different from me? Why was Nygard deemed the monster while he thought I wasn't one?

"I know my brother sees Nygard and I as the same, it is apparent. I won't let my brother win as he will do the same dark things as Nygard would for the one he loved."

"Then what are you going to do?" Jack asked.

"End all of this once and for all. All of it, not just this place, but any pain that any person has ever felt. I want to rewrite history, I want my human father back."

This felt like a moment where a normal person would start tearing up, but after so many years of not crying, of hiding my emotions, I just felt cold.

"You have a point, Cadi, but how are you going to achieve that?"

I shrugged. "We will see."

Chapter 16

I made Jack walk back to his own apartment near his pub instead of walking me back to my hotel. There were a couple of reasons for this, the first one being I wanted some time alone to ponder things. I wasn't that thrilled that Jack had told them about Nygard, even if he had a reason for it. I felt betrayed, as he could have told me. But he didn't, he didn't even try to communicate with me about it.

Was my father right? Should I be careful in trusting him?

Maybe I was making a big deal out of nothing. It wasn't like this changed anything, as my brother always thought I was a monster. I guess I was so used to having my secrets kept from people, that any time information about me got out to anyone, I became defensive.

The second reason I didn't want Jack to walk me back to the hotel was because I needed to figure out what I would do about a bike tomorrow. I had a feeling Nygard was already on it, but I couldn't be too sure. I knew I should communicate with him, but with so many emotions going through my mind at the moment, I was afraid he would find out about what happened and give me a lecture. That was not something I wanted to deal with at the moment.

To be honest, he probably already knew I went to punch Alan in the face, as I was a lot like him. If someone was going to screw me over, I was going to screw them right back. He would have killed Alan if he were me, but I knew I couldn't. Then there would be no way to reverse everything that had happened.

At least, that was what Jack and I had decided.

It was his idea, as I wasn't sure what I wanted yet. Being told I was a monster repeatedly by my brother made it a little harder to want to help him out, or anyone for that matter.

And the power Nygard spoke of sounded tempting.

As a car slowed down next to me on the street, I remembered the third reason I didn't want Jack to walk me home: because Kane was keeping tabs on me.

The car didn't stop or roll down windows to talk to me, so I kept walking, like I hadn't noticed it. I stayed on alert, however, just in case it wasn't Kane and it was another group of men who wanted to take me out. Even if I had a busted ride, as long as I found a new motorcycle, I could still compete.

Finally, the car stopped and one of the windows rolled down. I sighed as I stopped and turned to the car.

"Miss Ryetirf, will you please come with us?" The car door opened and what was apparently one of Kane's henchmen gestured me to come inside. He didn't have to use his gun, as he knew full well I couldn't refuse the request.

It wasn't like I would put up a fight against Kane in his own city.

I got in, sliding across the leather seat next to one of Kane's henchmen. He was muscular with very white hair, but not the kind that came with age. He appeared as if he was born with it. He had light blue eyes and had a glacial smile on his face as I strapped myself in.

"Thank you for not putting up a fuss."

"Why would I cause trouble for the man who might offer me a job?"

"Oh, you would be surprised at the things we deal with. Now, would you like a drink?"

I did, in fact, know the things he dealt with as I had worked with Jack quite a few times. Also, a drink after everything sure sounded good. "Yes please."

The man poured some whiskey in a glass, careful not to spill any on his beige three-piece suit as the driver set forward. He handed me the drink.

"Thank you."

He said nothing as we made our way down the street toward Kane's office. I thought about how many times I had been in the building now. It was quite a few times, which I wasn't sure what that said about me. I guess I just made very interesting impressions on people, and those people liked to either know more about me or take me out altogether.

Yeah, that about summed it up.

The rain was picking up and I could see thunderclouds beginning to form. I was glad this storm happened after the races as it would have just been even more miserable driving on a motorbike. Especially while getting shot at, almost run over, etc.

At least the crowd would have been very entertained.

Glancing over at the henchman, I always thought it funny how either they were very talkative or very quiet. There was no in-between. The talkative ones seemed to stop trying to talk to me when I came to Recar for Jack, however, as they found out I didn't like small talk. The quiet ones were always my favorite.

After about fifteen minutes, the car stopped in front of the office. The henchman quickly got out and opened an umbrella as the rain was coming down hard now. He came over and opened the door for me, keeping me under the cover of the umbrella.

If there was one thing I could count on for the henchmen of the leader of Recar, it was that they were chivalrous. Until they became your enemy. Then all bets were off and any method was up for grabs.

Which was why I never pissed them off. Except Damian, Jack's arch-nemesis.

The man led me into the building and a man took the umbrella from him to dry it off. He nodded to the man, as if words were not needed.

He was my favorite henchman by far, even if his cold, dead smile was eerie. I also didn't want to ever cross him, as he was probably one sadistic man.

I wasn't sure if that made me like him more or not.

"Empty your weapons in this box," he unlocked a box for me. "You will get your belongings on your way out."

I did as he asked, emptying my two guns and two knives into the box. He quickly locked it and led me to the elevator. Punching in the level that Kane was on, we headed up.

As the elevator dinged and opened, I noticed the receptionist was gone. I wondered for a moment why that was, then lost interest right away. Maybe she was just on her break.

The henchman opened the door and Kane quickly got up and lifted his arms, as if celebrating.

"There's our girl! Our star of the show!" He clapped. I could feel my cheeks get a little red. It was embarrassing having him clap for me with only one other person present. The henchman didn't seem to budge, though.

I still wasn't sure why he wanted me here. Did he just want to talk about the race and how ridiculous I had driven? Or did he notice something was up? I shrugged. "I'm not so great. I ruined my bike."

Kane waved his hand to the henchman. "Leave us."

The white-haired man nodded and left us to be alone. After the door closed, Kane looked at what I was wearing.

"Oh, this won't do, you need something better than that to wear."

I looked down at my jumpsuit that was riddled with bullets. "I didn't have time to change."

He went over to a dresser and pulled out a dress shirt and pants. "These will be a bit baggy, but I think they will do. You can change in that bathroom over there."

I didn't argue with him, as I felt he wasn't going to let this go. I also didn't want to him to see exactly how many bullets were on my jumpsuit because he might have even more questions.

After changing quickly, I came out of the bathroom with his baggy clothes on. This felt familiar, and it reminded me of the few times I had shown up with bloody clothes to Jack's office and he made me change.

"Much better. Now," Kane went to his desk and pulled out a file. "What do you think of this?" he asked as he handed it to me.

Curious, I opened the file. It was specs on a car. A nice car, with a turbo engine and everything. "It's a nice car."

"It's yours."

I peered over the file at him. "What?"

"Your bike was ruined and you need something new to race, right? You could go find another bike, it wouldn't be hard, but I want you to race in this car and show me what you are really capable of."

My mouth dropped a little. I didn't see this coming. A bright flash of lightning made me jump a little, followed by a crash of thunder. The storm was getting stronger.

"I can't accept this."

He waved, as if he was trying to say it was nothing. "No, it's the least I could do. Just having you in the race has boosted my ratings and made more people watch this tournament."

Kane paused as he stepped closer to me. There was another flash of lightning. "Although, if you felt you need to pay me, you could answer a few questions I have."

I knew this was coming, but I wasn't sure which questions he would ask. "Like what?" I tried to sound innocent, but we both knew I was far from it.

He smiled. "Oh, where to start. Let's see, first, who was in your hotel the other night? And where were you right before my men picked you up?"

I had a feeling he would ask about my whereabouts, but I didn't expect him to know Jack was over. Jack wasn't as stealth as he thought he was. "First off, who I fraternize with isn't any of your business. But if you must know, he's a local boy that I had met up with while I was around last trip here. As for who I just met up with…" I bit my lip. "The Republic racer tried to kill me and I wasn't going to let that slide. Can you blame me?"

Kane sat down and reclined back in his chair, bringing his fingers to a temple. "You realize we have a strict policy about our racers going after each other during the event, don't you?"

"That I do, but can you blame me? He broke my bike and tried to kill me. Asshole deserved it, is that not the Recarian way? Besides, you know three men tried to kill me the other day that were part of the races, and that I retaliated. You didn't seem to have a problem with that, now did you?"

Kane laughed. "That was self-defense. Had they survived, they would have been severely punished."

He paused again, turning to watch as another lightning strike hit a neighboring building, the sound shaking the floor that we stood on.

"If I'm not mistaken, you hit something in the road, did you not? How was it that Republic general's fault?"

I paused. Shit, I didn't think about what I said. "Because he ran over my bike. He could have avoided it. And avoided me."

Kane moved over to his desk and took a seat, scratching at his stubble. He gestured for me to take a seat.

I did not like where this was headed.

"You know," he said as he tapped the table and looked up at me. "I watched the replay of that video and the amazing reactions you pulled over and over again. They seem almost… inhuman." He leaned back in his chair. "Hell, even with the bulletproof jumpsuit, you should be in the hospital right about now."

I knew I couldn't deny that. If I lied, he could just go to the bathroom and look at my jumpsuit.

I let out a naïve laugh. "What, are you going to call me an angel that has fallen from heaven, or some other cheesy line?"

He made a half grin. "Normally I would, but in this instance, I am being serious." He stood up and looked out the windows, watching as the storm raged on. I stayed quiet, not sure where he was going to take this, not to mention it looked like he was trying to stay calm.

"You know," he started. "The rest of the universe may see us Recarians as uncivilized." He turned to me and smiled. "But we still know the myths of old—the ones that talk of a race of superhumans; the Sanshlians."

Shit, seriously? He was a lot smarter than I gave him credit for. I couldn't let him find out the truth, though, as it could jeopardize the mission.

I let out another laugh. "Are you serious? You buy into that fairytale crap?"

"I didn't, until I saw what you just did. And the fact you appear as if you didn't just roll across a street from jumping off a car going over 250 kilometers per hour. I don't care what physics you use, that does not add up."

"My suit is just that good, I guess. And the helmet. I've got a pretty good bulletproofed suit, very resilient against any bullets." Yeah, he wasn't that stupid but I had to try.

"Right. Let's say I believe you. What would happen, let's say…" He pulled out a gun and pointed it straight at me. "If I shot you right now. Would you heal incredibly quick? Or will your clothes miraculously stop the bullet. Oh wait, you don't have your jumpsuit on anymore."

So that was why he insisted that I change. He had thought all of this through. I had to give him credit, not many men were smart enough to put that all together, let alone letting something that was seen as fictional be part of his reasoning for his theory.

However, he had me cornered. If I said he was crazy, he would just shoot me to make sure. He didn't fear hurting me, as he had a few doctors on staff and knew where to shoot so it wouldn't be fatal. If I told him the truth, well, he would either shoot me just to see what would happen or not, or lower the weapon and want more information. Problem is, every scenario led him to the truth. I let out a sigh. This was such a long week.

"Fine. I am a Sanshlian."

He kind of stood there, surprised I would admit it so fast. Maybe he didn't even believe it himself, but couldn't quite grasp that it could be anything other than that. He lowered the gun and laughed.

"Huh, never did I think those stories were true. All these years, all these centuries, and there was really a planet out there with people like you. That is crazy."

He went back to his desk and leaned back, putting his feet on the top. "I have so many questions I know you probably won't answer. But I want to know, why would a Sanshlian be in the midst of all this drama?"

I had to be careful what information I would give him. He couldn't know about the trophy. "That, Mister Hulligan, is classified. But you can imagine it is why the Imperials and the Republic is looking for me."

"But why enter the races? That makes little sense. What do you have to gain?"

"I have nothing to gain—more just trying to find my place in this universe. The Sanshlians are a dead race, it isn't like I can go home, and between the Empire and the Republic, both want to use me for this stupid war. I was hoping I could hide on this planet, but there is nowhere I can hide, now does it?"

Kane pondered on the information I told him. It wasn't exactly a lie, but it wasn't all the truth. "Then why didn't you bolt the moment you realized both the Empire and Republic were here looking for you? That stunt you pulled probably confirmed their suspicion."

I shrugged. "Now where will I go? This was the last place I could hide. To be honest, I hoped that if I could impress you, then maybe you would keep me safe from those wretched people."

He let out a laugh. "It was one thing to let you dispose of the men that were after you, but now to find out why they are really after you, I'm not sure I would want you to stay. I don't think they would ever stop coming after you."

"With enemies around every corner, I would fit right in, wouldn't you say so?"

"That is fair." He tapped his fingers on his desk. "But I will have to admit, finding the truth about you being a Sanshlian might make that worth it."

I didn't want to resort to this, but I needed him out of my hair for the time being, and needed him as an ally because he was the only one who could keep me in the races.

"If I win, I can protect you unlike anyone else. As you see, I have a fast reaction time and not afraid of getting harmed for another's sake—especially since I can heal quickly."

He grinned from ear to ear. "That's what I like to hear. Well, don't worry, the car is all ready to go and will be waiting for you in the morning. My men will escort you back to your hotel. And remember, the race isn't until dark tomorrow and there is supposed to be a storm worse than this one."

With that, he escorted me out of his office.

Chapter 17

I wasn't sure if I should be happy about how that ended or concerned. I felt like that could be my future self's problem and for the time being, I could just be happy that I could get a car, and that Kane was letting me stay in the races.

So it all went pretty smoothly, I guess.

Kane's men took me back to the hotel after letting me get my guns and knives. It was the same white-haired man who had brought me in that night. He didn't say a word on the ride to my hotel, but gave me notes to where the car was being held, which was the same place my bike had been at. I decided I would go check it out in the morning since the races were in the late evening, which Kane had mentioned.

I could not wait to see what he had in store for us.

Now that I had a car instead of a motorbike, I would have to focus more on maneuvering around the corners and around people instead of getting run over. Easy peasy.

Jack was going to be pissed when he found out Kane gave me a car, not that I cared at this moment. I was still mad that he told my brother about Nygard, and I wasn't sure if I could trust him or not.

Also, Jack was going to be even more pissed when he found out I told Kane I was a Sanshlian. I would just leave that part out, I guess.

I got back to the hotel, thanked Kane's men, and went to order food. As I waited for a waiter, I saw that the overall count of points were being presented on the TV. Jack and I were tied with Logan in second place. Tim and Alan had no way of winning first, unless Jack, Logan, and I all got below fifth place, which I doubted was possible.

With Jack and I even on points, getting second would be easy. I just had to let him beat me in the next race. He would think he beat me fair and square because he was just that cocky.

As long as nothing unexpected happened, that is.

The waiter came, and I was able to place my order to have them deliver it to my room. I made my way up to the room, ready to unwind. I also wanted to change into clothes that actually fit me, though I would be lying if I said Kane's clothes didn't smell good. It was similar to what Jack used to smell like when he was ruler. Did all the rulers here just use the same cologne? Maybe it was some lucky formula or something.

I unlocked the door and noticed something was off. The room was dark, but I could sense something inside. Why hadn't I noticed it earlier? Usually I was good at these things. I had a long day, though, and didn't think more things could go wrong, so I no longer had my guard up. I scanned the room and saw a figure of a man sitting on the couch.

"Karovs!" I commanded out at the figure, sending ice straight for him. The figure responded with a word and swung out his hand. The attack vanished, and I could finally see who the intruder was.

I let out a breath. "Oh, father. I didn't expect you to be in here."

He stood up as I turned the light on. "And you attacked without checking to make sure it wasn't your love. How did you know it wasn't Jack in your room?"

"I just knew. Besides, that attack would have just winged him."

Father chuckled. "I see."

I took a closer look at him. It had been a couple of days since I had seen him, but I noticed that he seemed more disheveled than normal. His hair was usually messy, but it was more like a styled mess. Right now, it appeared he had run his hands through it many times. Even his eyes seemed a little red.

"Why are you here?" I asked. "Didn't we agree that we wouldn't meet up until after this was all over?"

"I came to talk about the race today. You could have been seriously hurt."

At first, I thought he would scold me, but he just wanted to make sure I was okay. Now I could put everything together—he was concerned about my wellbeing. Other than Jack, I wasn't used to someone wanting to make sure I was all right. It was strange to me.

"I'm fine. I'm a Sanshlian after all. A minor bike accident won't hurt me."

"You were shot at and could have gotten run over during those roundabouts."

"But I stand before you, fine and dandy."

He pursed his lips, as if he wanted to argue with me more, but had given up on it. Even with all his concerns, I had proven how well I could handle everything going on. Not only did I have years of skill under my belt, I was also trained to use the powers of the Sanshlians now. I was nearly invincible.

Nearly.

If I had listened to my mother, Violet, none of this would have been possible. Heck, I would have been maimed, or if a car ran over my head or heart, I would be dead right about now.

So, who did I actually trust?

"Where were you? What are you wearing?" he asked as he sat back down. Looked like he wasn't going to be leaving anytime soon.

I looked down, forgetting I was wearing Kane's clothes. I sighed. "Let me go change really quick and then I will explain." But I definitely wouldn't tell him the entire truth. There was no way I would tell him I told

Kane I was a Sanshlian. I did not want to see my father angry at me, even if it was something I had to do to keep my skin, so to speak.

"Go ahead." He gestured to the bathroom.

It was right then did I realize the only clothes I had to change into were my street clothes or my pajamas that were more than likely Jack's pajamas. After such a long day, I really wanted to change into my pajamas, but I also didn't want my father to see me wearing another man's clothing.

Then again, I was doing just that at the current moment.

I changed into my street clothes because I did in fact care. It was weird, I had grown up for so long with no father figure that it wasn't something I thought I had to worry about.

I came out of the bathroom and took a seat across from my father.

"So, where did you go?" His arms were crossed. Oh man, was this what little kids felt like? Is this what I missed through my preteen and teenage years? Is this what Dennis had to deal with? I did not like it.

"I obviously had to go punch Alan in the nose. Threaten him a bit."

Father pinched the bridge of his nose. "Myra…"

"He used his powers to try to run me over! He almost cost me this race!" I tried to defend myself. It clearly wasn't working.

"We could have just dealt with him after the races. If Kane saw you, then he would know you have a connection with them. Surviving what had just happened would have been all for nothing if you were seen."

I looked away, not wanting to meet his eyes. I could feel his anger rise.

"Myra... Look at me."

I looked at him and gave him my most innocent smile.

"What happened?"

A knock on the door made us both jump. "Room service!"

I got up and answered the door.

"Hello again, miss. Here is your order. Just leave the cart in the hallway when you are finished."

"Thank you." I nodded and he left.

I placed the plate on the table and started digging in. I was famished.

"Myra... You aren't going to get away with ignoring my question."

I put the fork down and sighed. "Kane picked me up after I left my brother's place and asked a few questions..."

"Like *what*?"

I shrugged. "Just what happened, I guess. I didn't give him any information, just that I was a trouble-causing girl that got in some sticky situations with both the Republic and Empire." I did my hardest to hide the truth. "That's it. Oh, and he gave me a new car because he wants to see how well I can drive a regular car instead of a bike."

He watched me closely, and I was afraid he would

read my mind to find the truth. He promised me he would never do that without my permission, but he seemed a lot angrier than normal.

"Fine. Just promise me you won't do anything stupid again."

"Well, I can't promise that, let's be honest here."

He cracked a brief smile. "You are too much like me. You are a wild one and that will get you into trouble one day."

"Oh, it has gotten me in a lot of trouble, but I find it to be a lot more fun that way."

He got up and looked out at the storm that was still lighting up the city. "You know, your mother always warned me not to do anything stupid or it would get me into trouble. I never listened, of course. Then everything that happened after I found the book..." he trailed off.

I didn't know what to say. The person whom he trusted most betrayed him and hid his one and only child so that he couldn't use her—use me.

But he wasn't using me. He was just teaching me what I could do.

"Do you trust him? Jack, I mean."

We had been over this, yet he always seemed to bring it up. I guess I couldn't blame him—he didn't want his daughter to make the same mistake that he had.

It was a question I have also been pondering all night. I trusted him to do what he thought was right and to help me, but sometimes what he thought was right wasn't what I wanted. When my brother and I were looking for Sanshli, he had joined us because the

Emperor threatened me. Although I am glad he had come, I still had to face the fact that he had betrayed my trust and was helping the Emperor.

Then he told my brother about Nygard.

But did I still trust him? Yeah, I supposed I knew he would never betray me in a way that would bring me actual harm. Or at least, he didn't think it would. That was never his intention.

"I do. He would never betray me."

He turned and faced me with a sad smile. "Good. Partners that wouldn't betray us are far and few in between. Keep him around if he is that worthy."

"He is."

"Is that why he is staying with the Republic? Because you trust him to gather them to Sanshli? Then you can gather everyone on Sanshli and restore the future?" he asked with sudden coldness.

Well, this took a bad turn.

I bit my lip, not sure how to answer. Nygard took my silence for a yes.

"Are you going to try to kill me, daughter? Will you take a knife straight into my heart and pull it out? Just like your mother tried to do?"

I quickly shook my head. "No, I would never do that!"

He started shouting. "Then why are they here? Why are you letting them have a chance at getting the gem?"

"Because I don't know what to do next!" I yelled back.

We both were quiet for a moment. I glanced out the window again. The lightning seemed to die down for a moment.

"It was easier this way—then my brother was where I could see him. Otherwise he would be terrorizing citizens of a planet that hasn't done anything wrong yet."

He raised an eyebrow. "You care about people that have nothing to do with you?"

I shook my head. "No, nothing like that. It's just that I can't stand him doing whatever he wants. Call it sibling rivalry, I guess."

"But what of Sanshli? Are you going to tell them where it is?"

I bit at my lip. "What... what is awaiting us on Sanshli?"

"What do you mean?"

I thought about telling him the dream I had, then decided not to. "Nothing, I just mean what happens when we go there? What are we doing? Do we go to the past? The future? All of this is a bit confusing and overwhelming."

He wrapped his arms around me. "I protect you, that is what we do. I will give you part of my power—the power of immortality. Then you can do whatever your heart desires."

It felt weird having him hold me this way. He cared for me—his daughter that his wife had taken away.

He backed away. "But if you let our enemy go with us, they will try to stop that power and more than likely try to kill both of us. Is that what you want? To be a martyr?"

I shook my head. "No. I don't. And I don't want you to die either."

He smiled and patted my shoulders. "That's a good girl. I better get back. Who knows what Joss has gotten up to since I have been gone."

I let out a little laugh. "I agree with that."

He ruffled the top of my hair. "Now get some rest, you have a big day tomorrow."

"I will try," I said as he closed the door behind him. I collapsed on my bed and cursed to myself. What kind of trouble had I gotten myself into?

Chapter 18

Dennis met me at the garage so we could go over the details of the new car. I saw him before he saw me and I snuck up behind him. It originally wasn't on purpose but then I noticed he didn't know I was standing right there so I waited. He turned and issued a rather high-pitched scream.

"Sorry, I didn't mean to scare you," I say with a brief smile.

"I'm just glad no one else is here, they would have made fun of me for that." He turned to the car. "Now let me give you the details of my 15700Z Racer."

I doubted it was his *racer*, but I didn't doubt he knew more about this car than anyone else on Recar. He went over everything, and I did mean *everything*. It was more than I ever wanted to know about a car, but now I was stuck with the knowledge forever taking up space in my brain. At least when I was racing, I could think about how exactly the mechanism from the foot pedal made the car accelerate, or how the brakes worked. Because that would totally come in handy.

Yeah, probably not.

But I let Dennis go on. It was a free car, and I was able to stay in the races. I could endure two hours of him talking just for that.

Yeah, two hours. Or so.

What was important was the add-ons. I was so glad there were add-ons. It also answered my suspicion about the leaders of the planet actually wanting boosters in the races, even though it was technically against the rules.

"This button will pump what I call 'liquid lightning', into the electric engine which will cause a ten second boost. And it will speed up fast so make sure you brace your neck. You don't want to get nasty whiplash."

"I will keep that in mind." Not that I had to worry. I would be fine.

Dennis put his hands on his hips. "That is it. I am sad about your motorbike, though, I really enjoyed working on that."

"Yeah, I miss it too. But it will be good to race in an actual car and show these guys what I am really made of."

Dennis nodded. "Yes, I am curious how well you will do in a car. And you have one of the best I have ever seen. But it still takes skill, not to mention there will be a storm tonight. Who knows what Mister Hulligan has in-store for you all."

I was curious as well, and with the storm, it would be even more chaotic. I couldn't wait.

The news said it would be the worst storm of the year, and with how large the one was last night, I couldn't even imagine. Normally, I would like to watch the storm, especially with Jack, curled up in his office with a cup of hot cocoa. I wouldn't get to do that, though, but be right in the middle of it.

What could go wrong?

"Anything else you need to teach me about the car?" I asked, even though I thought it impossible. He had taught me a lot over the last couple hours.

He stood there for a moment, looking up as if it somehow helped him go through his entire brain. "Nope. I think that is all of it."

"Well, thank you again, Dennis, and I hope I don't completely total this car." I held out my hand.

He shook it. "Same."

I checked the time. I still had at least three hours before the races started, and two before I needed to set up. I debated on what I should do. I could go beat on Alan some more, but I figured that would be more trouble than it was worth.

But his defeated expression would be priceless.

Deciding to get everything ready for after the race ended and the award ceremony, I headed back to the hotel. The award ceremony would start late that night, and I would want to rush out of there with the gem before Jack figured out what happened. I would also need to coordinate with Nygard what we were going to do.

I sighed. Why did it always seem like there was so much to do?

The ceremony will begin at 10pm tonight. Do you think you can have the ship and everyone who isn't in the races ready to go by 10:30? I connected with Nygard.

Yes, but what if you don't get first and Jack is able to beat you? How much time will you need to get the gem from him?

Don't worry about it. I will get the gem and meet you at 10:30. The awards don't take long since they'd rather party than have a lengthy speech and everything. Even if Jack got it, I could retrieve it and get to you in time.

I am trusting you.

I wasn't sure if he meant to get the gem, or that I wouldn't let Jack know the location of Sanshli. *You can count on me. I know what I must do to keep my life secure, and to live the way I want.*

I am glad to hear you have come to your senses. We will finally be able to make this galaxy the way we want.

I didn't care about the rest of the galaxy, I just wanted to be with Jack and live our life. It was all I ever wanted.

Arriving back to the hotel, I packed up all my belongings. I could have just left them there, to be honest, since I had more sets of clothes over at Nygard's hotel, but I found that the clothes Jack had picked out for me were quite comfortable and I wanted to keep them.

After that was all done, I lugged my bag to the street level and found an IK.

Handing him the luggage and a note, I said, "take this

to this address."

I gave him a few coins, and the kid ran off. That would save me the hassle of having to go to the hotel myself, especially since I didn't want to see Tim anytime soon. But I would have to deal with him that night. Ugh.

Having still an hour left, I decided to see if Jack wanted to grab a light snack before our set up time.

Jack?

Yes, my love?

Want to grab a bite? And maybe some tea?

Of course. Remember that café we used to go to?

That existed in this era?

Of course. It's Recar. Things never change.

That was for damn sure.

The café he was referring to, Café Diem, was a small café near the edge of town close to the area where the races would start. It always had the best scones and sandwiches, along with tea. I had a feeling Jack would order at least three pots because he didn't know what flavor he wanted, and then he was going to drink it all.

And be hyper for hours.

Jack was already waiting for me when I came up to the café. He gave me a hug and kissed my forehead. "Missed you."

I smiled. "You saw me yesterday, there is no reason to miss me."

"Any time you aren't with me, Cadi, I am missing you."

I blushed a little as we entered the café. I wasn't worried about being spotted, mainly because today was the last race and it wasn't like we couldn't fraternize. And besides, it was clear Kane knew the two of us were together. Jack, or Xander in this life, was a local. It wouldn't be weird for us to be an item.

Taking a seat, a waitress with a rather short skirt, handed us some menus. Jack thanked her, and I watched to see if his eyes lingered on her. They didn't.

Looking through the menu, I noticed that a lot of the items seemed similar to the ones in the future, but none were quite the same.

"Know what you want?" Jack asked.

"I think so."

He signaled the waitress over. "I will have a Monte Cristo sandwich and can we get a pot of the Earl Grey, Irish Breakfast, and Jasmine." Jack turned to me with a smirk. "And she will have the cream cheese and green onion jacket potato."

I stuck my tongue, even though he was right. He knew exactly what I would order. To be fair, I knew he would order three pots of tea. Now I would have to deal with caffeinated Jack at the races. Great.

"Now, why did you invite me out this afternoon?" He asked as the waitress left us. I shrugged.

"Just wanted to talk. We don't get to often."

"Talk about what? Yesterday you were quite pissed at me and now you are all smitten. What is going on? What happened?"

I licked my lips. "Nothing happened, okay? I am just glad I had you to watch my bike. I don't think I would have survived yesterday if it weren't for you."

He shook my head. "Nah, you would have figured something out, you always do."

"Yeah, but it probably would have involved more bullets hitting me and it would have hurt."

"Fair."

"But I'm serious, you do always have my back, even if I don't deserve it."

Jack reached forward and grabbed my hand. "You deserve it, Cadi, don't let your brother say any different."

I smiled. That wasn't what this was about—it was about what my father had said, but I didn't know if I could really explain. "I just have had some time to think about everything, and with the last race coming up, and our return to Sanshli, I wanted to make sure I said it."

He watched me closely, as if watching for some clue for why I really was saying it.

"You are just being nice so I will let you win."

I let go of his hand and gave him a look. "Uh, I don't need you to let me win, because I am a better racer than you."

He leaned back, "Maybe on a bike, I have to admit, you have more room to maneuver, but in a car, there is no way. I will beat you."

Rolling my eyes, I responded. "Sure, whatever. We will see, now won't we."

The waitress put down the three pots of tea. I still couldn't believe he was like this, and yet I still loved him.

"What kind do you want to start with?"

I didn't enjoy having caffeine so late in the day, but since I would be leaving the planet that night, it probably wouldn't hurt. "I will take the jasmine, but just one cup. I'm not some crazy tea fiend like you."

He let out a laugh. "Tea fiend. I like it. Better than 'Crazy Jack'."

"I think is part of the reason they call you 'Crazy Jack'. That, and the clocks." I bit my lip, debating if I should say it. "You know, Kane collects spoons."

Jack looked up from his teacup. "You went up to his office again?"

"I was forced up there, yes. And he collects spoons. I'm not sure which I find stranger, but I feel that spoons are less annoying."

He jabbed his finger at me. "Hey, people like clocks! They tell time!"

"No one likes to know what time it is, Jack, just admit it. It's creepy."

"Well, if you had to collect something, what would it be then?"

I paused. I had never given it much thought. "Weapons. I would have a bunch of torture devices in my office to scare anyone who comes in."

"You know, I almost didn't see that coming. But it makes sense. It makes perfect sense."

We laughed as the waitress delivered our food. The potato had steam coming off of it and looked delicious. I wasn't sure when the last time I had a jacket potato like this was. It was simple to make, sure, but since I rarely made my own food, and ate in the cafeteria on Anosira, I only could choose between what default options they had. All they had for meatless options was some kind of tofu. Real original.

I really did not like tofu.

"So how do we want to go about tonight?" Jack asked as he took a bite of his food.

I poked at my potato, waiting for it to cool down some. "I don't know, I guess whoever wins will get the trophy and then we meet up after to take it out, then we decode it before the others find us, then split up to meet at Sanshli."

"Sounds easy enough."

I took a bite of my potato. "Yeah, but it never ends up being that easy, you know that."

"I think we will be able to pull this off though, unless there is something you aren't telling me?" He watched me closely, and I made sure to shield my mind from him.

"No, there's nothing else."

That was a complete and utter lie. I wouldn't meet up with him to get the gem, and I wasn't going to decode with him. I would take it straight to my father and we were going to go to Sanshli to finish what he started.

And I would be the second most powerful being in the galaxy. Then Jack and I could be together wherever we wanted with no one to stop us.

Jack and I finished our meals, and the rain started to pick up. I guess the storm was coming after all.

In more ways than one.

Chapter 19

The storm was raging above the city and I could barely even see the car parked in front of me, which would be Logan I presumed. I couldn't even tell anymore.

And the fact it was dark made it even worse.

The city lights magnified with the rain made it harder to see out of the windshield. If one thing was for sure, I was glad that I wasn't on my bike. There was no way I would have been able to ride in this. Or at least, not without using my powers.

Lightning crashed down around us, hitting the street somewhere in distance. The cracking thunder followed mere milliseconds after. This would be oh so much fun. I had never been afraid of the weather until now.

Well, maybe that one time on Ttkas.

Civilians were running off the track. I squinted to see

the red light beginning to flash. At least there were no idiot civilians on the sidelines tonight. Even they were smart enough to stay out of this mess and watch from the surrounding buildings. Any of us could slide out of control and hit them.

You ready, Cadi? Jack asked me via the link we had.

As ready as I will ever be.

I mean after I win this, because you screwed up so bad last time, what will you give me in exchange for the trophy? I have come up with a list of things I believe to be of equal value—

How about I just promise not to scar that pretty face of yours?

Oh, kinky.

I rolled my eyes. I knew he would say something like that.

Be careful not to roll your eyes while driving—it can be dangerous. Especially in this weather.

I will try. What about you? Will the idea of what I will exchange be too distracting for you?

Actually I think it will be a better motivator.

I laughed. *Sure it will be.*

Don't worry, I'll prove it to you. See you at the finish line.

With that, he dropped the connection. It would be hard to let him win after all that cocky talk, but I couldn't let it deter me from what my goal was.

To win second place and get out of here as fast as I could.

The red light flashed again, and we all revved our engines. Thunder boomed again, distracting me temporarily.

I prayed to whatever god there was out there that Kane didn't make this track as hard as I thought he would.

The light turned green, and we were all off. I passed Logan with ease and was even with Jack as we headed straight towards where the storm awaited us.

A gigantic bold of lightning hit the ground in front of us and it took every effort I had not to close my eyes from the blinding light. The thunder shook my car, but I pressed forward. Lightning didn't hit the same spot twice, right?

The first corner we turned, I honestly almost missed if it weren't for Jack turning. I followed him, heading down a small, one car-width alleyway. This area seemed familiar to me, but with the rain I couldn't quite place it.

Why did it feel like we were going somewhere I didn't feel great about?

As we got out of the alleyway, I remembered what it was. We were heading towards the docks. And in this storm, the docks would not be a safe place for cars.

Glancing behind me, I found someone on my tail. All I could make out were headlights. If I had to take a guess, it was probably Logan. Turning forward, I kept my eyes on Jack's car. He was the only one out of us who knew these streets like the back of his hand. I had a feeling for this round, just like the last, I should let him go first.

The first part of the docks was easy. It was all paved and had a barrier between the water and us. Although the waves were trying their hardest, they weren't quite making their way onto the roadway.

The second part, however, was a completely different story.

The road was no longer asphalt, but made of wooden planks that were not at all designed for cars going at this speed. My car shook as the tires hit the wood. I swore one of them cracked, but I pressed on, and paid more attention at the waves that were heading towards the dock.

Why was it always water?

At least this time I was in a car and not a bike. I would have already been a goner.

One of the waves hit Jack and I and I pressed the gas a little harder, trying to make my way through it. I could feel my car start to be dragged towards the edge of the dock and I quickly turned it inwards back towards the city.

There was no way I would let this ocean take me down with it.

After a couple of minutes of battling the wood and the enormous waves hitting us, Jack led the two of us into a new alleyway. I let out a breath I had no idea how long I was holding and looked forward to what would happen next.

When we came out of the alleyway, I was not expecting what they set up for us.

There was an entire street carnival set up. There were no people out, of course, but did Kane expect us just to take it all down with our cars, or dodge all the stalls? Because they were really scattered. And I mean *really* scattered. For some reason, they weren't arranged in a straight line like normal. I weaved around them as best as I could, taking out one or two on the way.

Jack didn't hit a single one. I was rather impressed.

I glanced behind me to find Logan hitting half a dozen things before getting in the groove. I could only imagine what chaos Tim and Alan were causing.

Which would just make more chaos for later.

We rounded the next corner to find the line to start the next lap.

I wasn't sure if this was easier or harder than the last round. It was shorter, that was for sure, but with the storm looking as if it was about to get a lot worse, I could only imagine what waves were awaiting us at the dock, and the stalls were now scattered throughout the street, causing even more disturbances.

It was an everchanging arena with nature holding the strings. My favorite.

During the straight stretch that led into the storm, I passed Jack. I didn't need him leading the way any longer as I understood what this race was about.

I did still almost miss the first turn as blinding light coming from the lightning strike that lit up the street. With the rain also acting as a giant wall across the windshield, it was lucky I didn't clip a corner of the building.

And I had no idea if anyone else did.

All I could see behind me were headlights as I drove down the alleyway. I presumed it was Jack, as he was the last person I passed. I also doubted Logan had the acceleration or maneuverability for getting pass Jack.

Jack was a lot better driver than him, on top of just knowing this city well.

And he could read minds so he could predict where most of the racers were going.

I had my mind shielded, a perk of being an Illusionist, so he couldn't use that power on me. If I didn't, however, I wondered if he could have figured out where I was going, and whether he would have used it against me. In that scenario, I would have called him a cheater, which makes me think he wouldn't have done it. He would have wanted to beat me fair and square.

Now I was on the calm part of the docks. Although there was a barrier, I could tell the sea was getting even more restless, and parts of the waves were seeping over the top of the wall. This was rather concerning, since the waves had no real barrier up ahead.

My powers would come in handy here very soon.

The first wave threatened to swallow up my entire car. I tried not to scream as I lifted my right hand and commanded them to bypass me. And Jack. I didn't particularly want to have to go and retrieve Jack in this, so I made sure he was safe amid all this chaos. Then Logan was behind him, whom I didn't worry about—he had the power to control water. As for Alan and Tim, I really didn't care. I hoped they got swept out to sea. Then I wouldn't have to deal with them anymore.

I, however, knew I wouldn't be that lucky.

Thank you. Jack said in my mind.

No problem.

The wood on the dock was not happy that we were

coming around for a second time. The car shook more than it did the first round and I wondered if it would hold up, or if we would fall into the sandy water underneath us. I tried to examine my surroundings, to see if there was a way to bypass it all, or if there was an area more solid than this, but I couldn't see far from the area right in front of me.

Besides, if Jack hadn't used a better section than this in the first round, then there probably wasn't a better section.

Turning down the alleyway, I prepared for the next area. I presumed the cars and booths would be scattered across this section, as cars has clipped them or ran straight into them. Although in most instances, I knew my car could take it; I felt that there could be traps in some of them, like bombs or something. You never knew with these people.

Maybe that was why I fit in so well.

As I turned around the corner, to my surprise, a lot more of the booths were still intact than I thought there would be. The best way to get around them was to drift, but with as much water as there was on the streets, drifting with control would be near impossible.

That is, if I didn't use my power.

It wasn't cheating if I just used my powers just a tad, right? That was what I kept telling myself, anyway. It wasn't wrong; it was using my assets I was born with. Yeah, that was how would I put it.

So it was drifting time.

The car slid as I used all my efforts to get it to slide

exactly where I wanted without hitting any of the booths. Glancing behind me, I saw Jack doing the same. Except he wasn't using his powers, he was just that good.

I would have him show me how to do that in this much rain sometimes, although I didn't particularly want to drive in this rain again.

That was, if I decided I wanted to go back into the future. I mean, I did, but I had the realization that the whole universe, and timeline, was open to me. I could go back to the time when I was supposed to be alive—the distant past when the First Empire was first created. Or I could go in the distant future and forget about anything and just be with Jack. I could find an era where there was no war, but only peace.

But would that really make me happy?

I shook my head. I had to focus. This was not a time to start thinking about Sanshli. There would be time for that on the ride there, as it would take several days to get there. Then I could ponder all the things I wanted.

Yippee…

I could see the line starting the last lap. Now I just had to figure out where I would let Jack pass me. I still had the booster, and I really, *really* wanted to use it to see how fast this puppy could go. But there was also the fact that the road was so wet that it would probably cause me to crash.

There was only one way to find out.

The storm raged on; the lightning striked all over the road right in front of us now. I could even smell the ozone. This was the most intense storm I had ever seen. I just wished I could enjoy it more.

Then the one thing I didn't think would happen... happened. A strike of lightning hit straight into my car.

I should have seen this coming, but I was just so amazed by the storm that I didn't. Luckily, the cockpit was not affected, and I didn't just have a billion joules of energy go through me.

But my engine did.

The car slid across the water, dead.

Shit. Shit. Shit.

Cars flew by me, turning down the alley way.

Shit. Shit. Shit.

All I needed was fifth place. If I could just get this car going, I could catch up. I started hitting buttons. Nothing was responding.

Shit.

That's when I remembered what Dennis talked about, and how the engine worked. If I could just recharge it, get energy to go back through it, then I could go. Just like the booster.

If I could harness part of the lightning, I could put enough energy in it to get it going again, then with the booster I would be able to get at least fifth.

Thank goodness there was enough rain blocking the cameras and the prying eyes of other drivers that I could hide what I was about to do. And damn, this was going to hurt.

I rolled down the window and concentrated with all the energy I had. I didn't need a full lightning strike, as that overpowered the engine already. No, I just needed a sliver.

When the lightning struck right next to the car, I reached out and called part of it to me. My other hand was on the console, ready to direct the energy. As the fragmented lightning entered my body, I yelled out in pain.

This hurt a lot more than I could ever imagine. But the car started.

I took a deep breath, letting my body heal itself, and stepped on the gas.

As I entered the alleyway, I gained up on the last car that had turned in front of me before I got the car up and going again. Once the alleyway opened up again, I was able to pass that car and three others before the docks turned into the wooden panels. I couldn't use my booster yet as It would just take out the wood. I had to wait at the right moment while going through the fake market.

And just pray that I didn't hit a booth that had a bomb.

I used my powers to deflect the waves. I really didn't care if anyone saw me at this point, as I doubted they could in this storm anyway. Maybe the cars closest to me, but they were so focused on what they were doing, I doubted they would pay me much mind.

I had no idea what place I was in currently, as I couldn't even see the car markings. I figured the best bet would be to keep passing people until I could only see one light ahead, and hope it was Jack. It was the only plan I could think of.

I came up to the markets and hit the booster, letting my powers guide me through. I saw in the distance ahead a giant explosion. I was right, some booths had bombs in them. I just hoped it wasn't Jack, though I knew better.

I passed at least four more cars and could see some lights in the distance. There had to be at least three cars ahead of me, but I couldn't be sure if that was all of them. The finish line was just up ahead, and I was already using my booster.

Maybe I still had some energy left...

I placed my hand on the console, a shock passing through me and into the car. Then the car jolted forward.

I passed one more car and went across the finish line. I just hoped I did it.

Sliding to a stop, I jumped out of the car and ran to the rankings.

Third. I had gotten third in this race. I collapsed in triumph on the ground, the rain already soaking my entire outfit.

I had done it. I had gotten second place overall.

Chapter 20

I never liked banquets.

I mean, the ones on Recar were a lot better than the ones Neil made me attend. At least here I didn't have to wear a fake smile. I enjoyed the people on Recar a lot more than any of the sycophantic representatives Neil had over.

The only problem with this banquet was that Jack was going to get very jealous of Kane. Although Jack won, it was still up to Kane to pick who would be his next driver, and he could hire more than one. I had a feeling he would discuss it with us tonight, although it didn't matter—Father was readying a ship so when I got the map, we would be ready to go. Everyone was with him, other than Tim and Logan. They were both racers so they came, and also to make sure I did nothing rash. I mean, they never said that, but I could tell by Joss' glare that he still didn't trust me. Didn't blame him, no one should trust me right now. I didn't even know what I would do next.

I wore the violet dress that Kane had sent over in the package containing the note "something to match your gorgeous eyes." Yeah, he was going to cause trouble tonight, especially considering Jack hated him all ready. It was a beautiful dress, though; the color really did match my eyes. It had a strap over the right shoulder and a slit that went up my left thigh, a little higher than I liked, but I was used to that. At least I had more freedom with my legs if need be. The dress itself went down to my ankles and the rest of it fit just perfectly, even the white strap heels. I particularly didn't care for the fact he guessed my measurements, but given where we were, I wasn't surprised. Jack did the same thing when I won the races all those years ago.

Jack was waiting downstairs in the lobby of my hotel. I was surprised to see him, especially since I thought the goal was to not seem like we knew each other. I supposed it was a little late for that, and the fact that after the next few hours were over, it didn't really matter.

"What are you doing here?" I whispered as I took the arm he was offering.

"Well I figured since we came in first and second, and were so close, that we should go to the shindig together," Jack emphasized the word "second", making me sigh. He wasn't going to let it go, probably ever.

"Does Kane know? I have a feeling he sent a car for me

already and will be very confused when I don't show up for it."

"I saw the car and talked to the driver. He knows."

"Of course you did. What, did you suspect that Kane would come get me himself?"

Jack smirked. "Maybe I get a little jealous, can you blame me? You always go after those persistent bad boys."

"Can't say you are wrong, can I?"

"Ah, she admits she likes it. By the way, I really like the dress you are wearing. Where did you get it?"

"It was a present from Kane. Reminds me of the dress you got me when I won. He even got my measurements right, just like you did."

Jack let out a slight laugh. "Well, you always do make a magnificent show. No one can keep their eyes off of you."

Jack opened the door to the town car and gestured for me to take a seat. I slid into the car and he went around and got in on the other side.

Now what I really wanted to talk to you about... Jack said through our connection. *What is our next plan?*

What do you mean? You won the races so you will get the map and save the universe.

I'm being serious, Cadi, what is your plan?

I didn't answer for a moment. I didn't know what my plan was yet as I didn't want my brother having the map, but I didn't trust Joss or the others either. Then there was Dan...

Cadi...

I don't know, okay? I don't trust anyone, I don't think anyone is in the right. What am I supposed to do, Jack?

Do what is right, Cadi.

And what is that exactly? How do I know what is right? My brother is going insane and killing innocent people because he is paranoid, meanwhile my father has been kind and nice to me, teaching me how to use my powers. How am I supposed to believe he is some evil man of the stories when I wasn't there to witness what happened? When all I have seen is his good side?

Cadi, he's a monster. You know this.

Is he, though?

What?

I mean... Jack, he has taught me everything I've ever wanted to know. He doesn't treat me like shit, but as an equal. Who am I supposed to believe when I've been treated so kindly by him?

Cadi, he killed his own people. He destroyed an entire planet, then went after the rest of the galaxy. He's so powerful that he couldn't even be killed but was trapped in stone. You know this.

Those are stories though, told by one side. The Sanshlians treated his people, the Illusionists, like garbage and didn't let them use their powers. I mean, what would you do in his situation?

Jack didn't answer. I wasn't sure if it was because I made a valid point or if it was because he was disappointed with what I said. We stayed quiet for the rest of the ride.

The drive to the ballroom was uneventful, which I was thankful for. I honestly was expecting something to happen, as it always seemed to. As we arrived, I could see the party was already underway with many women dressed in beautiful gowns and men in tuxes. They looked like little flower petals dancing in the wind. Jack got out and opened the door for me and held out his hand.

"Now, doesn't this bring back memories?" He asked with a cocky smile.

"Of you being a creeper? Yes."

He laughed. "But you love me for it."

I didn't answer but leaned in and kissed his cheek. It was rare for me to see Jack surprised, but his eyes widened.

"What was that for?" He asked, almost suspicious.

"Nothing, just that I want you to know out of everything, I care about you the most."

"Now you really are scaring me. What's going through your head?"

I shrugged. "I just don't know what's going to happen next, and in case I don't get to say it, I wanted to tell you that."

"You mean the world to me, Cadi, but also, I'm not giving you the trophy."

I gave him a look and elbowed him in the stomach. "That's not what I was after but thank you for the clarification."

"Hey, I'm sorry. It's just weird for you to actually say something like that. Usually it's just when you are trying to get something you want."

That was fair and very true, as I had been doing just

that to Kane.

Jack and I entered the building and made our way through the crowd, talking to those who wanted to congratulate us and talk about our skill. Most of the other racers ignored us as they were pissed that we won by so much. Even with my sabotage, I was able to get second, and many didn't like that. The fact that Kane sponsored another car made it even worse. So most of the other racers ignored us, which was fine by me—I honestly didn't want to talk to any of them.

"Ah, my two best drivers standing side by side." Kane approached us with a smile. "I didn't know you two knew each other."

I glanced at Jack. "We have talked a little during the races. We were so close in points we had to get to know each other."

Jack smiled. "A sexy woman on a bike, how could I not introduce myself?"

Kane gently grabbed my hand. "I concur, she is as impressive in person as she is on the tracks. I'm glad she showed up for this tournament, although I have a few racers to choose from. All of you did very well."

"But even with all her talk," Jack glanced at Kane holding my hand, "she didn't get first."

I shot Jack a look. "If that accident didn't happen, I would have destroyed you in these races."

"But you weren't even in a car, you were in a motorcycle. That defeats the purpose of these races."

Kane raised his hand. "Please, please, no need to argue here. You both did very well, and I was able to see what everyone is capable of. Now, please enjoy this party, I know I will. Myra, would you care for anything to drink? Some food perhaps?"

I nodded. "Yes, that sounds lovely."

Sorry Jack, but we have to go with this, just for tonight.

And you get mad when I flirt with my lady staff, geez.

I ignored his comment and walked with my arm through Kane's. We went to the food table, and Kane made me a small plate of food.

"So, I'm still interested in your story, and what exactly you can do. I have this feeling, however, that I'm wrapped up in some other plot that's going on, and I am going to get fully screwed over."

I almost choked on my champagne. "You think I will screw you over?"

"Am I wrong? I have to admit, I'm pretty pissed that my racing stars are all going to leave even though I spent money sponsoring them and the trophies and all that. I mean, there really isn't anything stopping me from detaining you all since you all have double-crossed me."

"Why are you saying this to me? I mean, if you really thought that, wouldn't you not say anything and just arrest me here and now?" I asked, sipping my champagne.

He shrugged. "And ruin this party? No, that would be no fun at all. Besides, I enjoy seeing you in the dress I picked out."

I blushed a little. "Ah yes, I meant to tell you thank you. The color is beautiful."

"My pleasure. Now, please entertain me for the night.

As I have a feeling you are going to disappear."

Smiling, I nodded. "Yeah, I can do that. Just lead the way."

Kane led me out onto the dance floor, his right hand wrapped around my waist while he put his other hand in my right hand. "I presume you know how to waltz?"

I, unfortunately, did. "Yes I do."

You are going to dance with him? Really?

I ignored Jack's comment and let Kane lead me as the song began. He was quite skilled at dancing, just as I thought he would be. It seemed like that was a prerequisite for being a leader of Recar, as there were always dances like this where the leader would need to impress a girl. At least that was my theory.

Kane didn't try to move his hand down my waist and remained a complete gentleman. Maybe he realized Jack was the man who had snuck into my room a couple of nights earlier, or at least that was my guess. He could also just be an actual gentleman. I heard those supposedly exist.

"So, where will you go from here?" he asked me as he twirled me out and then back into arms.

"Oh you know, somewhere across the galaxy, causing destruction and chaos in my path."

He laughed. "That sounds about right. Will you be looking for that legendary planet?"

I bit my lip, debating on what information to give him. "Perhaps. Why, what do you want to know?"

Shrugging, Kane gave me an honest look. "I just wish to know more about this legend. It's not every day you find out these fairytales are real and such."

He was right on that part. "Let's just say we might be."

We danced a little more, not saying a word. The song ended, and everyone clapped.

Kane grabbed my hand and kissed my fingers. "It was a pleasure meeting you, Myra. I feel sorry for you, though."

I looked at him a bit quizzically. "What do you mean?"

"All your searching, and you seem like a person who will never find their home—where you truly belong. I wish you luck, though, and hope you find it someday."

With that, he left me standing there. I was surprised at his comment, but knew it was true. I probably would never find my home in the way he was saying. I glanced over at Jack, who was talking to some girl. Once my eyes adjusted, I realized it was the woman I had talked to at the bar the other night. Small world. She was probably someone's companion for the evening.

Logan stepped up next to me, a drink in hand. "Is everything ready to go?"

I nodded. "Yup."

"You didn't win first place, though."

"Don't worry about that. Just accept your third-place trophy and meet me at the entrance over there." I pointed at where I was talking about.

"If you double cross us, I will destroy this entire place and everyone in it."

"Chill," I said with a little smile. "Or I guess you are the king of chill, since you control ice and everything."

He gave me a look, then walked off. At least I didn't

have to talk to him anymore.

It was time for the trophy ceremony. I could feel my heart racing. This was the moment I was waiting for—this is when I would have to decide what I am doing.

Cadi, are you ready? After the ceremony, meet me in your hotel room and we can figure out the code from there.

That wasn't what I was going to do. Jack thought he had the map in the bag, but that wasn't the case.

Yeah, that sounds good.

He was going to be so pissed. Honestly, I wasn't sure if he would forgive me for what I was about to do. I was about to make a run for it to the ports and fly off with my father.

Because I trusted him.

He has been the only one who has been upfront with me, the only one who was able to tell me the truth of what was going on and how to use my powers. If I helped him go back, he could teach me even more and I wouldn't have to obey anyone's command ever again. I wouldn't have to live out the torture like I had in the past.

"Third place goes to Peter Haas!"

The crowd went wild. I wasn't sure why, it wasn't like any of them knew him.

"Second place goes to Myra Ryetirf!"

Everyone clapped. I quickly turned to Kane. "Goodbye and thank you. If I make it out alive, I will come back, but don't get your hopes up."

He gave me a slight smile, but I could tell he was pissed still. I went up to the stage to collect my second place.

"And first place goes to..." The announcer spoke as I started back down from the stage. I walked as if I was going to my table. "Xander Vanguard!"

Just as I expected, everyone stood up to clap for him. It was chaotic and perfect for sneaking out of here.

Before anyone realized it, I used my powers to pull out the gem. I showed it to Logan, and he had a slight look of surprise and then annoyance on his face. As we started out of the banquet hall, I handed the trophy to the woman I had talked to at the bar.

"Take it. Do whatever you want with the money," I whispered in her ear.

Then before Jack finished taking his trophy, Logan, Tim, and I were out of there.

Chapter 21

We got out onto the sidewalk and only a slight drizzle falling from the skies now. I was very glad the storm had stopped.

"So you lied to everyone. What a surprise," Tim commented as we started running down the street. We needed a taxi, but I didn't see any around.

"How about you shut up and we find a way to get out of here before everyone else finds out that I lied? Or is not having cocky remarks impossible for you?"

Tim said nothing as we hurried down the streets. The odds were low that we would find a taxi.

Which just meant we would have to hijack a car.

As we passed an alleyway, I noticed there was a car parked to the side of the roadway. Perfect timing.

"This car, get in."

Tim tried the door. "It's locked."

I punched the driver's side window out and unlocked the car for him without a single break in eye contact.

"Fine, whatever." He got in and Logan took the front passenger side.

Getting in, I used a little magic to start the car. It rumbled to life. I backed out and floored it down the street.

Logan looked like he was holding on for dear life. "Don't you think you should slow down? Aren't the cops going to come after us?"

"Nah, they are at the banquet. You will notice there is a lot more crime tonight than most, as the citizens know this fact as well."

Tim bent forward so he could be heard. "And you liked spending time on this crap-hole of a planet?"

"Yeah, because you weren't on it." I replied. Even Logan chuckled at my comment a little.

The space port was on the other edge of the city, of course, and I knew a lot could happen between here and the port, as it always did. I just prayed that a little more time would pass before Jack would realize I was gone and would come after me.

Father, do you have the ship ready? I asked him.

We are close. It won't be too long. Did you get what we need?

Yes, and I have Logan and Tim with me.

I am proud you didn't leave them behind. And Jack?

I paused, wishing I wouldn't have to say, or think, the answer. *I left him behind. He would have jeopardized this mission. I will just make it right after we go to Sanshli.*

That's a smart girl. Be careful who you trust, and you will live much longer.

I just hoped he was right.

We will be there in fifteen minutes. Be sure to have everything ready as I'm not quite sure if Kane will shut down the port, or if my brother is already there waiting.

Understood, and I will keep a look out.

Thank you. I will keep you posted if there are any problems.

I kept my speed up, going a bit faster than the surrounding cars, but not enough to deem it dangerous, at least not for me. I had a bit of an upper hand compared to the drivers around me, as I was a Sanshlian and a professional driver. Not many could get away with the driving I was pulling off. And by the look on Logan and Tim's faces, they didn't think I could pull it off either.

As I rounded a corner, I found an entire street blocked off for construction.

"Son of a bitch," I mumbled and turned around to head down another street. This would add at least a couple more minutes to the drive. I guessed it couldn't be helped.

"Do you know your way around here?" Tim asked.

I shot him a look in the rearview mirror. "What?"

"You do in the future, of course, but this isn't the same planet as it is then."

I let out a laugh. "This planet has not changed its layout, or at least not by very much. Believe me, I know how to drive in this city."

"Whatever."

I tried to ignore Tim for the rest of the trip. I didn't need his shit talk anymore.

About halfway to the port, I heard Jack trying to communicate with me. *Cadi, what are you doing? Where did you go?*

I'm sorry, Jack.

But you don't have the map, you have... Shit, Cadi, what did you do?

Jack...

Cadi, please don't do this. Don't give into him. You aren't him. You aren't evil!

Never claimed to be perfect, Jack.

Cadi!

I'm sorry. I love you.

I forced Jack out of my mind. I didn't want to hear what he had to say anymore. I could feel a tear escape the corner of my eye.

"What's wrong?" Logan asked, just quiet enough so Tim couldn't hear him. I knew he did that on purpose and I was thankful for it.

I shook my head. "We've just got to hurry, they will come after us soon."

"Then step on it."

I did just that, pushing the car a little faster than we were currently going. Tim bounced a little back and grabbed the handle. This made me laugh and forget for an instant what I had done.

I had betrayed the only man I had ever loved.

Trust worked both ways, and I had broken that equal exchange. I wondered if he would ever forgive me for all that I was doing just so we could have a life together. Was I making the right choice? Or should I stop right here and now to go back to him and do what we agreed to do?

No, I knew in my heart that this was the right choice. I had been training with my father for a while now and I didn't believe he was a bad guy. He just had to make decisions that were forced upon him. He wasn't as dark as everyone said he was.

As for Joss and the others, well, they were the only ones on Nygard's side. Although I didn't want to work with them, I didn't have a choice. When the time came, I knew I could leave them behind and do what I wanted to do.

And that was run away.

We were coming upon the port now and I didn't see any signs of the area being grounded for the time being. This was a good thing, and Kane hadn't decided he was done with my shit. I wouldn't have blamed him if he did, as I had lied to him quite a few times. He knew I would find a way off this planet either way. I was pretty resourceful.

Abandoning the car in the parking lot, Logan, Tim, and I raced up to where my father was waiting for us. The ship was, of course, on the other side of the port. It always seemed like every time I traveled, I had to walk all the way across the port, no matter what planet I was on nor what planet I was headed to. I wondered what the odds of that were.

Joss and Nygard were in the cockpit, doing checks

with Jane in the engine room, making sure all was ready to go. I helped Jane in the engine room with the last check and we closed up the bay door to head to space.

I held on as the ship moved up and forward towards the deep blackness that made up the universe. It was strange that with everything that existed, there was a lot more of the black nothingness. I felt there was more to it —something scientists didn't see, but that wasn't my field. It was just a hunch I always had while looking out at it.

Once we had stabilized, I stood and made my way to the cockpit to talk to my father. As I entered, he turned to me.

"Well done getting the gem. I had worried since you didn't get first, but I see that worry was for nothing."

"I didn't know what I wanted, so I didn't tell anyone it was in the second-place trophy, not even Jack."

"I'm glad you didn't trust anyone with that knowledge, it means you are learning to keep yourself from being betrayed. Good job. Now wait for me in the mess hall and we will take a look at the gem."

I didn't say anything. I didn't know if I wanted to side with my father, or if I wanted to keep my word with Jack and bring everyone back to Sanshli to restore the universe without Nygard's rule.

This entire time I could feel Jack trying to communicate with me, but I had kept blocking him. I didn't want to talk to him, as I felt I would not like to hear the words he had to say. He was more than likely pissed. I was afraid he would say the words I never wanted to hear from him: I don't want to see you ever again.

It would be my fault, I knew, but I couldn't let this opportunity pass me up. I had to take fate by the horns and embrace it. This was who I was supposed to be—an Illusionist capable of unlimited power.

At least, that is what Nygard kept telling me.

Chapter 22

I sat in the messroom, twirling the stone in my hand. Shining a light on this would give us the information we needed to find Sanshli. With father looking at it, it would be easy, as he could decipher the letters and all that in no time.

What my father was doing right now, I wasn't sure. He told me to wait in here, but that was an hour ago. Was he just flying the ship, or was he meeting with the rest of the crew about me? And if so, what were they discussing? I knew the rest didn't trust me, which I couldn't blame them, but what did my father have to say about me? Was he just telling them to behave?

Either way, all of it made me feel very uneasy.

I decided not to give it much thought. I was screwed either way, as I couldn't escape the ship. I just had to remember my father wouldn't betray me. At least, I doubted he would. After everything that has happened, I trusted him to keep me safe. All of this, he said, had been for me. Violet, my mother, had hidden me for a reason. He had always wanted me and wouldn't let others hurt me.

At least, that was what I kept telling myself.

The door slid open and my father stepped in, along with the rest of the imperials behind him. Joss gave me a look but said nothing. A smile crept up on my lips. I liked the fact that he was still pissed at me but couldn't do a thing anymore, not when my father was now in control. He had given me so much abuse over the years; I liked seeing the tables turned.

Father held out his hand. "Let me see the stone."

I gave it to him, and he examined it. "Yes, I remember this. Your mother had it made so she always had a way to find our home. I was quite impressed as she didn't even use the Illusionist's book to create it. If only she learned with me, the two of us could have been unstoppable." He gave me a smile. "But now we can. I was so broken when she took you away from me, I knew you could achieve the same greatness I could, and so far, I have found that I was right."

I didn't know how I felt about what he said. I felt glad he found me worthy of training and thought I was powerful, but what did that mean exactly? What did he want with me, and why was I so important to him? And why did my mother think he was a monster? What was I really missing in all of this?

Placing the stone in a little box he had brought in, it projected the map on the wall. Symbols floated all around a center dot which I deduced was Sanshli. I glanced over at father whose eyes seemed to glisten.

"That's it. That's our home."

Home. I didn't feel I could ever understand that word. My child home was destroyed, then the Empire was never my home, and I never knew Sanshli. The only place I felt I could belong was Recar.

I pushed back those thoughts and the thoughts about Jack. I didn't need to come to that realization right now. I had to focus. I could ponder about Jack later.

"How long will it take to get there?" I asked.

Father studied the map a little longer and then went to the screen pad and made some calculations. "About a week, so not too far out. You know how the planet can move around the galaxy, disobeying the laws of physics."

I knew this, as my brother had searched for it for the better part of the year, sending as many men as he could to the area we had originally found it, but it was not there. "I am aware, since it wasn't where it was last time we found it."

"It was the Illusionists that were able to make that spell so that the planet could be safe from the rest of the galaxy, before they threw us into exile Our powers made them safe and yet they all turned on us. Doesn't seem fair, now does it?" My father was watching me for a response.

I shook my head. "No, it doesn't." And I meant that. It

didn't seem fair that part of a society that had been powerful enough to keep them safe, and do so much for them, were thrown into exile and treated like scum.

He placed his hand on my shoulder and smiled. "I'm glad to finally have someone see my point of view, everyone else was brainwashed and thought I was wrong. Except a few here and there."

He was referring to Joss' family—Neil's family and ancestors. There were some families that sided with Nygard, mostly to save their own skin. I didn't blame them, I have done enough in my life to save my own skin.

Was that what I was doing now? Did I deep down think Nygard was impossible to beat, and I had just given up? No, it wasn't just that. I really believed that maybe there was good in him—that maybe all the stories weren't true and that there was more to the tale.

"There shouldn't be anyone following us, so it should be easy to get the book we need. That is, if Arcadia doesn't betray us." Joss folded his arms as he glared at me.

I gave him a look. "How would I give them the info? I came straight here."

"Who knows, you and Jack seem to have a special bond. You might not even need to interact," Joss added.

That was true, but I hadn't let Jack back into my mind since I left. I saw my father give me a suspicious look. It would explain why I asked him for the spell to be able to talk through the mind at great distances. I turned away from him, not wanting to deal with that right now. I figured he already knew about it, as Jack was able to escape right after he taught it to me, but now he was putting together why I wanted to connect with him. It was so I could do the same with Jack.

"He didn't know the map was in the second place trophy, that was obvious when he tried so hard to beat me. I am not as open to him as you think I am."

He didn't reply as I had a point. The key reason why I didn't tell him was I wasn't sure what I would do myself, rather than outright trying to deceive him the entire time. I cared for him, but at this moment I was afraid he would try to stop me. I wanted to finish this and find the book. The idea of being able to control my own destiny— to have the power to not let anyone ever talk down to me or order me around—was enticing. I had been used and abused for far too long, and I was beginning to understand why Nygard did the things he did.

"I trust my daughter not to lie to me. We will head straight there and we will right the wrong that has been done to us. Neil and Jane, you can have first watch for the cockpit, as Logan, Tim, and Myra are probably tired from performing at the races. Any objections?"

No one said anything to my father. No one seemed to ever want to talk back to him, except maybe me from time to time. Right now, I didn't want him to suspect anything, especially since I had nothing for him to suspect me of, except maybe for Jack.

I retired to my room to rest for the night. It had been a long day between winning second, the gala, and the stress of betraying Jack. Jack had been trying to contact me, I could feel it, but I was still pushing him out of my mind. I hurt too much already to hear his voice in my mind. I wondered what he thought of me now. I would look for him after everything was over and explain, but right now I had to do this on my own. He didn't understand where I was coming from. After everything was said and done, then he would understand. Then we could run away and do whatever we wanted since I would have the power of the Illusionists—the power my father once had.

Lying on the bed and closing my eyes, I tried to push all thoughts away and go into deep sleep. I must have been getting good at pushing away feelings because a few moments later, I was asleep.

I was back on the planet. This time was different, though, as this time I had remembered the other dream, and I knew I was dreaming.

And I had complete control of my body.

I wandered through the forest, taking in everything about it, and not letting the twigs catch on my clothes. This was Sanshli. I could feel it. Everything seemed the same as when we first came here.

Except for the giant beast.

I was puzzled at why he wasn't in my dreams this time, and why the creature had changed in the dream. Last time it had been some giant, evil creature with tendrils that lashed out every which way. And this time, unlike before, it wanted to destroy the planet, not guard it.

Wanting to see the creature again, I started towards the waterfall.

As I reached the water, the same scene started to materialize. A creature came out of the water, its dark tendrils destroying everything in its path. It was nothing I had ever learned about in the Sanshli legend, not to mention it wasn't there the last time we were here.

What exactly was this thing?

Since I could now move, I decided to take a better look at it. There appeared to be something floating above it and I wanted to see if I could confirm whether my theory was right. I climbed around the waterfall, gaining the highest ground I could.

Then I could see him. Nygard.

He was the one in control of this beast. I couldn't believe my eyes. Or maybe I could.

Turning, Nygard saw me and held out his hand. "There is nothing to be afraid of, daughter, this is what the world deserves."

I shook my head. "No, this is darkness—this is an evil force, even I can feel it."

"This isn't an evil force, Myra." He stepped closer. "This is me."

He took my hand, and I went falling forward, through the beast, and into the water.

Gasping, I found myself back on the ship. I was drenched with sweat and took a few deep breaths. Everything was fine, it was just a dream.

A dream with images relaying harsh truths I needed to confront.

Chapter 23

I never thought I would be where I was at the moment.

I mean, I was alone in the mess hall, which was normal for me, but it was strange to be on a ship with Nygard, heading to Sanshli. I had kept telling myself that it was for the best and that Jack would eventually understand after I gained the power my father promised. Then we could be happy and hide somewhere for as long as we wanted.

At least, that was how I thought it would go.

Jack was forgiving most of the time, so I had a feeling he didn't completely hate me, but I didn't know how well he was at running away and hiding. I had always thought that was what he wanted, but with everything that had happened, he almost seemed like he wanted to fight for this galaxy, and do what he thought was right.

What was right, though?

I didn't have an answer to that question. I had seen the things the Empire has done, but I had also seen the things my brother had done for what he thought was "right". I didn't believe either of them were good, so what could I do?

As I sat there, sipping my cup of peppermint tea, Nygard walked in, interrupting my thoughts. I glanced over at him, not sure how I should greet him. He was my father, but he was also the leader of the entire galaxy.

Or so he used to be.

He grabbed himself some tea at the automatic drink machine and sat down across from me, blowing on the freshly brewed tea.

"You seem deep in thought. Do you want to talk about it?" he asked. I wondered if he had read my mind or if my face was really giving away more than I wanted it to.

I sighed. "I just don't feel I know what is right."

He took a sip of his drink. "Is this you saying this, or is it the ideas Jack put in your head?"

He knew me far too well. "I just don't know if taking the Imperials with us was a good idea. How do I know they won't betray us in the end? Like they did last time with me?"

"They won't betray you, not this time."

"That doesn't change the fact they have committed innumerable horrors through the years—the horrors that I took part in."

Nygard took my hand. "You are not evil. Those were things you did to protect yourself. I can relate."

I bit my lip, debating on asking him the question that had been on my mind for some time now. "What exactly happened? On Sanshli, I mean."

He took a deep breath and let it out slowly. "I guess I should tell you everything that happened. I am not proud of what I did, but it had to be done."

Nygard straightened up and took another drink of his black tea. "I grew up in a small caravan. There were about ten families overall that traveled throughout Sanshli. We usually stayed on the outskirts of the city, set up camp, and entered town to do simple tricks for money. I always grew up hearing how we were an abomination and how the Illusionists weren't good for anything but some entertaining tricks.

"Back then, the only powers we could do were the equivalent of a human circus act. And I honestly thought that was all we could do. That is until I stumbled upon that book."

He paused, as if trying to find the exact words he wanted to say. I could tell he was still angry about the way his people were treated, and everything that had happened. I would be too.

"The book not only held the history of the Illusionists, but spells and instruction on how to use our power. We weren't some pathetic group that couldn't make real magic work, but powerful beings that had once ruled the entire planet. All the structures, all the safety precautions that were in effect so the rest of the universe couldn't find us, it was all because of us. You can imagine my anger."

I could, as he wasn't doing a good job at hiding it at

the moment.

"I then hid the book as I didn't want it to get into the wrong hands. I had a suspicion it was the last one in existence, and I wouldn't let anyone destroy it." He licked his lips. "I trained with it for a while and when I felt powerful enough, I told the first person I thought would understand. The one person I trusted. Your mother.

"She didn't think it was a good idea for me to train, but to leave things be. I tried to explain to her we needed to do something—this couldn't be the world we let our child live in. At that time, you were about two. I doubt you remember any of it."

I shook my head.

"I didn't think so. She and I got in a big fight and I stormed off to the place I kept my book. I trained more and when I got back, the whole caravan was waiting for me. They wanted to kick me out. I tried to tell them what I could and what had happened to our people, but they didn't care. That was when I snapped. I burned down all the wagons, all of our homes. People tried to stop me, but I was more powerful than them. Only a couple caravan members survived and ran straight to the capital to alerting the leader.

"Men came for me, but they weren't strong enough. I was able to defeat them all. Then they sent more and pretty soon it was like an all-out war, but it was only me against all the people on Sanshli. Eventually a select few realized I was too powerful and sided with me. I didn't need their help, if we are honest, but it was good to see some people understood."

He was referring to Joss' family. I wondered how many others there were in the galaxy that had family lineage that was tied to Sanshli, or if it all had been diluted with regular human DNA.

"I destroyed all of Sanshli. I didn't mean to, but they left me with no choice. They would have killed me and destroyed the last book if I had done nothing. So it wasn't something I could just give up on.

"Your mother was still alive through all of this, hiding you from me. She fled and joined up with some human that had believed her." He paused, as the memories seemed to be coming back to him. "I didn't ever want to hurt her. I just wanted you to grow up in a place where your kind was accepted. I don't know why..." Nygard trailed off.

"Eventually she was able to somehow transport you into the future. I found it to be ironic because she was using the Illusionist power without ever having studied the book. She could have been so powerful, and yet she decided not to be. She did a good job hiding you, but fate brought you back to me. I knew it would.

"Meanwhile, I took over the planets and created the Empire. It was rather prosperous for quite some time until the human she had sided with came after me and somehow was able to lock me up in that stone."

All of that went along with the stories I heard growing up, but they felt different when he told them. I could understand why he did the things he did. They were told with his words instead of the words of the people who feared him.

But I still wasn't sure who was right.

Maybe no one was right, maybe the idea of good and bad was some made-up concept. There didn't seem to be a correct answer here and now I debated everything once again. Maybe the only good thing in life was just protecting yourself. But at what cost did that come? Father had destroyed an entire planet to protect himself, and I had done countless things as the Emperor's Shadow trying to save my own skin.

Perhaps I was just like him.

"Any other questions?" Nygard must have wondered why I was so quiet.

I shrugged. "It makes sense to me. But you talked of no one knowing where the book was. How then were they able to make you into stone next to it?"

He made a little smile. "You catch on. That wasn't the real book, that was a fake."

"What?"

He glanced behind him, making sure no one had entered the mess hall. "That book is a fake with a spell would kill anyone who used it. The real one is somewhere else on the planet—somewhere only I can get to. And you, when the time comes."

I couldn't believe what I was hearing. Neil was so close to killing himself. Damn it, why couldn't I be that lucky. "I'm glad I didn't use it then."

"You would have been fine. I wanted to make sure if you ever found your way there, that no harm would come to you."

I wasn't sure if that was satisfying to hear or not. Was I really the only thing he cared about?

He finished his tea and stood up. "It is almost my time in the cockpit. I presume you will be taking the engine room soon?"

I nodded. "Yeah, I guess I should relieve Jane."

"One week until Sanshli, and you will understand the power you are capable of. You have no idea how long I have been waiting for this moment."

I smiled but didn't say anything. I had a feeling I did.

I found Logan and Jane making out when I walked into the engine room. I coughed, letting them know I was standing there.

Logan was first to back away. Jane seemed like she didn't care I was standing there and would have kept going, making me leave. Typical of her.

"I believe Logan and I have the next shift?" I asked. "Unless you don't want to get some rest and just keep on going with that."

Jane gave me a look, then left the room without saying another word. I shrugged. "Suit yourself, I wouldn't have minded."

"Is it possible for you not to be a bitch?" Logan asked as he typed into the computer.

"No, I think it is impossible. Most of my life I have been around Tim, or Tom, or whatever."

This comment actually made him smile. Maybe I was getting somewhere with Logan, which would be weird. I didn't think that was possible, not that I really wanted it.

He and I were quiet for some time, as neither of us were the talkative type. Most of the work in the engine room was rather mindless, and my mind could unfortunately wander more. I hated it, but I hated small talk worse.

Jack had never stopped trying to interact with me and connect. It was like hearing a constant ringing in my head, and no matter how many times I tried to disconnect from it, I just couldn't. He wasn't getting the memo I wasn't interested in talking to him.

There was a slim chance he could figure out the exact location we were headed. He was skillful with reading minds, but I didn't think he could read mine so far away. I guess we would find out once we reached Sanshli and they showing up.

If they did, however, I doubted Nygard would let them land, not to mention he would kill everyone on board right then and there. Up until now, I think he was testing me and seeing what I would choose, but if push came to shove, he would kill anyone who got in his way. He had done it before, and I knew he would do it again.

As for Jack, I was sure he wouldn't hurt him. Jack wouldn't betray me, not in the way Violet did. I mean, he was trying to stop us, yes, but it was more about Nygard than me. He just wanted to make sure I was okay. There would be no way he would do what Violet did and stab me through the heart like that, both emotionally and physically.

I wondered if she knew it would just put him into a sleep rather than kill him. She put so much into place so that I could go back and destroy him. All that changed when my adopted father died. He would have trained me to hate Nygard, and eventually we would have killed him.

Funny how fate led me down a different path.

"You seem to be deep in thought," Logan commented. "Maybe talking out loud will help you solve your problems.

I gave him a surprised look. I never imagined he would ever try to see what was on my mind. "Excuse me?"

"You just skipped five steps on the log you are doing. I don't like seeing mess-ups."

Ah, I was messing up because of my thoughts. I let out a sigh. "Just going over everything that has happened so far in my life and how I was set up to take a certain journey, but that journey went to trash when I was little."

"Like how you were hidden from your father to destroy him, but you are now allied with him?" he asked. He must have heard the story.

"Yeah, something like that."

He pushed a couple of buttons. "Well, if you ask me, I say save your own skin, in whatever way that is possible. I mean, sure it would be good to go back to the future and pretend none of this ever happened, but I guess you don't actually belong there, now do you?"

I shook my head. "I don't know where I belong anymore."

"Well then," he tapped his tablet. "Maybe that's where you should start."

Strangely, he made sense.

Chapter 24

Our rotation in the engine room ended, and I went to get dinner in the mess hall. I ignored the fact that Tim was in there and sat at the opposite end of the table. Logan sat next to Tim, and I hoped their conversation would block anything Tim had to say to me.

I was wrong.

"You know," Tim began. "You did a wonderful job betraying that Boy-Toy of yours. I'm surprised you could be such a bitch, even to him. It's rather impressive, actually."

I knew I should just ignore him, but he was starting to get on my nerves. And I also was getting a lot better at my powers.

So, I flipped his plate of food right into his face.

He stood up, his rice and curry dripping off of his face.

"You bitch!"

His fist turned into a ball of fire, and Logan quickly stood up.

"Tim, no! We are on a spaceship! You can't use your powers!"

"Like hell I can't!"

He raised his fist, but Logan was quick to use his power, water and ice covering Tim's hands. I had to hold in my laughter. I didn't want him more pissed at me.

"What did you do that for?" Tim yelled at Logan, running his hands in warm water in the sink.

"You were about to make a big mistake, that's what." Logan sat back down and started eating his dinner.

Tim didn't respond, realizing it was true. I just sat there, keeping an eye on him to make sure he didn't do anything else stupid. It was Tim, so he probably would.

To my surprise, he didn't say another word and sat down and finished his meal. I kept my mouth shut as well since I didn't want to deal with him any longer.

Finishing up my meal, I went to my quarters to rest. I had a piloting shift in about six hours and figured sleep was probably a good thing. Laying down, I tried my best to not think about anything except imagining what life would be like if it weren't for all this mess.

And it worked, I fell right to sleep.

The black tendrils engulfed the entire planet.

I was no longer the only one on the planet, now the planet was full of citizens. They must have been the people who once lived on the planet, all of whom

Nygard had killed.

The people he was killing all over again.

He hovered above the beast, his eyes as dark as the tendrils that smashed down on all the buildings, destroying everything in its path. People screamed, mothers dove to save their children. This wasn't a war like he said, this was a genocide.

None of these people were fighting him, they were all innocent.

I ran to my father and held out my arms. "Father! Please! I beg you!"

But he didn't hear me, or at least he didn't act like he did. He seemed fixated on the destruction and didn't care what was in its way.

And in this dream, he didn't care I was in his way.

The black tendril went straight into my chest. I gasped, all the air leaving whatever air I had left in my lungs. But I didn't die, not yet anyway.

I felt the darkness consume me. It was like I was conscious yet not in control. I could see my hand lift up, dark lightning coming out of it. I was becoming him—I now had the power of pure destruction.

But I didn't want it.

I could feel myself crying as the blackness exploded out of me in every direction, destroying buildings, landmarks, statues, trees, life itself. I had no control. I was losing myself to the darkness.

Someone help me. Please.

There was a light shining down on me. It slowly came down and I could feel its radiance as it made its way before me. It was inches away, I could feel my redemption.

Then I felt something pull me out of my sleep.

I was gasping for air. This time I wasn't covered in sweat, but it felt like something had ignited all of my nerves and I was shaking uncontrollably and still trying to take in a full breath of air. I wasn't sure why it didn't feel like my lungs were filling, but I kept trying to breathe.

Was this a panic attack?

After a few moments, I was able to breathe again. Everything felt like it was calming down now and I didn't feel like needles were going through my nerves any longer. I wanted to scream, but I also didn't want people rushing into my bunk.

This dream had differed from the others. There were people on the planet this time, which was different from every other dream I had ever had. Was it just because of the story Nygard had told me the day before? But it felt so real…

The dreams I had before we went to Sanshli warned me of the beast, even though the beast was there to meet me and help me find what I was looking for. Did these dreams mean that there was a monster awaiting me on the planet again? Or was the monster supposed to be on this ship?

Was my father really the monster?

I couldn't understand why my dreams were trying to make my father out to be a monster when I understood why he had to fight. I understood why he did the things he did, and I agreed I would have done the same in his place.

Or was that why the darkness consumed me?

I checked the time with my pocket watch. It was about time to get up anyway. I sighed and changed. This was going to be a long shift, especially since it would be with Nygard.

I debated on telling him about the dreams. Would he understand why I was having them? Or would he think something in me subconsciously wanted to betray him?

I went into the mess hall and grabbed a bite to eat, and some tea to calm me down. I really liked the peppermint tea, but I decided to make some chamomile and lavender. I sipped on it, letting the taste calm me down a bit.

It definitely wasn't strong enough, but it was at least a little comforting.

After finishing my meal, and my tea, I made my way to the cockpit. Nygard was already there, surprising me. Joss was supposed to have the shift before us. Was I later than I thought I was?

"I decided to relieve Joss early, so you didn't have to interact with him." Nygard leaned back. "And there is something about watching space go by that is always comforting to me."

"Did you read my mind?" I asked this time as I was really tired of everyone reading my mind.

He shook his head. "No, I just know you well enough to guess."

I felt a little bad about my accusation, but knew he

understood. He had read my mind in the past, so it wasn't like it came from nothing.

I took a seat next to him and stared out at the stars. He was right, there was something about looking out at space that felt calming. I wish I could stay here forever and ignore everything that wasn't in front of me.

Glancing over at my father, I found him staring out at the dark void of space. I watched him for a moment, curious as to why he found it so comforting.

Maybe because the stillness of space didn't reveal the horrors a person had faced.

"Do you think the beast will be there?" I asked, not sure why I did.

Father turned to me, a little confused. "The beast?"

"Yeah, the shapeshifter that was guarding your statue. Brayen, I think his name was."

Nygard let out a little laugh. "Oh, that guy. I remember him. He had joined your mother and that human. So, he guarded Sanshli all that time? I pity him."

"What do you mean?" I asked.

"He devoted his life to keeping people away, so I wasn't brought back to life, but it was all for nothing, which I explained to all of them many times. They should have listened, and we wouldn't have to go through all this mess."

I never thought about it like that. I guess he really did waste centuries of time. "So, he's not there?"

Nygard shook his head. "No, in this timeline he's not. You don't have to worry about him."

I guess that was good, but there was still one beast I

wasn't sure of. "What about a beast made of darkness?"

He looked at me a little quizzically. "A what?"

"A beast that is made of shadows with large tentacles."

"There is no such thing on Sanshli. Why do you ask?"

I paused, biting my lip, wondering how I should explain. "It's just that I've been having weird dreams. It was about this large creature that was destroying Sanshli. I had never seen anything like it before, it was like pure darkness. Everything it touched was obliterated."

Nygard didn't say anything for a moment, as if he was trying to process this information. "How long have you been having this dream?" he asked.

I shrugged. "I don't know, just for the past few nights."

"And you are just now telling me?"

"I… I didn't think it was important."

"It is important. All dreams the Illusionists have are important."

"I… I didn't know. I'm sorry."

He let out a sharp breath. "It's fine, just make sure you tell me next time. I don't want you to have to suffer with them anymore. The Illusionists have always had dreams, omens they called them. They aren't the best to have, but they have saved my life more than once."

I had always had nightmares my entire life. I never thought anything of them, as usually they were about the same thing over and over again. The first ones I knew were because of my connection with Sanshli and that I needed to find it, but since then I thought they were just mainly memories and fears.

Never did I think it was part of being an Illusionist.

"Now, tell me, what exactly happens in the dream?"

I let out a sigh before going on. "It has changed each time, but mainly I am on Sanshli and I come to this lake with a waterfall and as I approach it, a creature that is like just a bunch of tendrils comes out of the water and smashes down on the planet, crashing all over, and destroying everything in its path."

Nygard seemed quiet for a moment, then asked. "What else?"

"Y… You are controlling the creature, or more that it is controlling you."

He nodded, as if knowing that was what I would say. "What changes between the dreams?"

"The first time I had no control over my body and it led me to the lake. It was all forest, and it was just me. The second time I had control and could go to the lake of my own free will. The third time the city was inhabited by its people, and we were in the city. In that one the creature struck me and it absorbed me into it."

Father rubbed his face. Was he frustrated with me or was it something else? I fiddled with my fingers, not sure what to do.

"Your dreams aren't a premonition. Someone is using you, trying to make me out to be the bad guy. I don't know who, or well anyone that is alive that would be capable of this. It could be just a bunch of ghosts from the afterlife and they are trying to seek their revenge on me through you."

He turned forward and looked out at the space that

laid before us. "After our shift, I will teach you how to shield yourself from such attacks, something I should have done a long time ago. I just didn't know they were still that powerful to get to you and for that I am sorry."

"It's fine," I said as I turned to check the readings. Everything on the ship was fine, but one could never be too careful. "I'm just sorry I said nothing sooner."

"And I understand. You still aren't sure if I'm the bad guy or not. I get that, daughter, as all the stories are about how I am a monster. I don't blame you for being cautious, in fact I commend it. You never know who you should trust."

I felt a little bad for him to feel that way. He really had lost all trust in people, yet he still seemed to trust me. Why was that? Did he really care for me more than anything?

A few hours passed, and our shift was over. I stretched, wishing I moved around more during my shift. I stayed in my head so much that I forgot to get up and walk around as much as I should have.

As father promised, we went to the mess hall so he could teach me how to block myself from the dreams, or attacks from the ghosts.

"Sit down and close your eyes."

I did as he asked. I felt weird sitting there with my eyes closed, as I didn't like keeping my eyes closed around people, but I knew I could trust him.

"I want you to focus on all the energy that surrounds you."

It seemed silly to think about, but after having trained using magic for the past few months, it almost seemed natural now. I focused on the energy that made up my surroundings.

That's when I could feel all the spirits, just like the first time on Sanshli.

I started hyperventilating.

There were thousands, if not more, of shadows surrounding me, encircling me. I could barely see. I kept trying to catch my breath, but it wasn't there. Nothing was there.

"Focus on me, daughter, focus!" I could barely make out my father's words, even though I couldn't see him in front of me.

I tried to focus on him, but there were so many voices, and so many shadows.

"Repeat after me, 'kvir na frib vas'."

I opened my mouth, but nothing came out.

"Say it!"

"Kvir na frib vas!"

Suddenly everything vanished. I blinked. I no longer could hear their whispers or see them encircling me any longer. Everything was gone. I took a deep breath and let it out slowly. Tears started flowing down the side of my face.

They were gone. I did it.

"Myra, can you talk?" Father knelt down beside me and tried to place his hand on my shoulder. I flinched, and he backed off.

"I'm… sorry." I said. "I just don't want anything near

me right now."

"I understand, I just want to make sure you are okay."

"I'm fine. The ghosts are gone."

He smiled. "I'm glad. I am angered that they attached to you to get to me."

I didn't know how to respond. I didn't blame him for the ghosts. It wasn't like he sent them, but finding out they had been with me this entire time was rather unsettling.

But now they were gone.

"Thank you," I whispered.

"You are welcome. I am glad to have helped. Your nightmare problem should be resolved."

I just hoped he was right.

Chapter 25

The week went by and I didn't have any nightmares.

Nothing else happened either, other than Tim getting in trouble a few times when he tried to set me on fire. No one wanted damage to the ship and having a fire on a ship always spelled disaster.

So maybe I had been egging him on, but he always started it. If he just didn't talk to me, I wouldn't have come backs that would piss him off.

I had to admit, traveling with David was a lot more entertaining than these guys. I mean, I had my father, and he taught me some minor magic, but it wasn't as entertaining as playing cards with David. I thought about asking Logan if he wanted to play, but realized that would probably be a mistake. I wouldn't have meant anything by it, but I felt that Jane would be mad at me, and also, they were spending a lot more time together, anyway.

So, I spent my time alone, trying not to let my mind think of Jack. He was persistent, still trying to communicate with me in my mind. I never responded, although at sometimes I almost gave in just to tell him I was sorry, but I knew that wouldn't be a good idea. If I started talking to him, I would give in and tell him we were going. I couldn't do that. Not yet, anyway.

We were to arrive to Sanshli in the morning. I lay down in my bed, excited that in the morning I would see the planet that should have been my home—the planet I was born on.

It was so strange to think about.

I had always thought I was from Garvner and then was taken to the Kamps and had to survive there. That was my childhood, all of it, or so I thought. Then all of this was dumped on me.

I didn't know where my real home was.

Letting my thoughts dwindle, I was finally asleep.

And the nightmare came back.

This time it was different. We were back at the lake with the waterfall, except this time I was controlling the creature. I hovered above it, stretching my hand out, watching the land before me get destroyed. The darkness engulfed me, controlling my every being.

Then I saw the people below me, fighting.

It was the Imperials and my brother's crew who all had been thrown into the past. They were all there. I could feel the hatred for each of them rage through my body. I held out my hand, tendrils slashing down on them.

This is what they deserved. This is what they all deserved.

That's when I saw him—Jack.

One of the tendrils went straight into his heart and I screamed. He looked up at me, reaching his hand towards me.

"Cadi, I... love..."

He fell over. I let out an agonizing scream.

No, this couldn't be happening. This couldn't happen. I wouldn't let it.

I flew down to him, the creature still on a rampage, striking down the forest. I put my hand on Jack's chest, trying to bring him back.

Nothing was working.

I focused as hard as I could, giving my life force to him, but my energy wasn't transferring to him. I watched as it was being siphoned away from me and into the creature. Turning to the creature, I screamed at it.

"Stop! I must save him!"

The creature didn't try to stop, but kept on taking energy from me and from Jack. I turned back to Jack, tears flowing down my face. He lay there, motionless.

"Please... stop..."

I woke up, the tears in my dream now in the physical realm. How long had I been crying in my sleep? Why did the dream come back? Why was it different this time around?

And why was I not able to save Jack?

I sat up and took a deep breath. I knew it was probably a stupid idea to do it alone, but since I remembered the words father had told me, I checked to see if the spirits were back.

They were still gone.

So if it hadn't been the ghosts, then what caused the dreams?

I dried my face with my sheets and stood up, pondering this thought. Father had mentioned that Illusionists could dream of the future. Was this what awaited me on Sanshli? Was I going to hurt Jack?

No, there was no conceivable way that I would ever hurt Jack. I cared about him too much and would never let harm come to him. I promised myself that, at least. He would never hurt me, and I promised myself that I would never hurt him.

I checked the time on my pocket watch. It showed to be almost morning for standard time. We would reach Sanshli soon, and I couldn't wait. I wanted all of this to be over, the faster the better.

That way Jack wouldn't have time to find this place, if he could, and my dream would never come to pass.

I quickly changed and headed to the mess room to drink some tea to calm myself down. I would probably have more of the chamomile lavender tea as that had helped me a little earlier. When I entered, Joss was already sitting at the table.

Joss and I had done a good job not running into each other or interacting the entire time I was on the ship. I didn't have anything to say to him, and I think he was pissed he couldn't abuse me with his power any longer, as I was his leader's daughter. I was glad the tables had turned, but I also just didn't want to deal with him any longer. I didn't understand why my father kept these men near him, other than to be a buffer between him and anyone who stood in his way.

Maybe they were just human shields, in the end.

I got some tea and some toast. I wasn't that hungry but knew I should at least eat something. Sitting down on the other side of the table, I blew on my tea.

We were both quiet for a good few minutes, not even exchanging glances. I think we both wished the other didn't exist. Joss was the one to start the conversation.

"Never did I imagine that Nygard would be released when we fulfilled the prophecy."

I raised an eyebrow. "You mean you are saying you wouldn't have treated me so poorly if you had known?"

He let out a brief laugh. "Treated you poorly? I saved you."

"Because you figured out who I was."

"I could have just arrested you and kept you in a jail cell until I figured out where the planet was. But I didn't. I gave you a job and trained you to be what you are now."

"Oh?" I asked. "And what am I now?"

"A cold-hearted monster. Just like your father." Joss let the word 'monster' linger. I couldn't believe what I was hearing—he thought Nygard was evil, just like in the stories, and yet he still followed him. It made no sense.

"You think my father is a monster?" I asked slowly.

He shrugged. "We are all monsters, aren't we? It's the only way to survive in this world, I have found. But yes, he is a monster. He destroyed an entire race. I shouldn't be living knowing that my species was destroyed—my home. Our home. My mother and father told me countless stories of him and of our home world. My ancestors only sided with him to survive. You only live because he cares about you. You have lied to him countless times and normally he would kill for that. Yet, here you are—alive."

I wanted to stand up and slug him, but I felt that would prove he was right. My father and I had no patience for anything. We just resorted to violence.

So maybe he was right. We were monsters.

"I do wish I told you earlier, though, then I wouldn't have had to deal with all of this and we would have found it a lot sooner. And I wouldn't have had to deal with you getting close with Jack."

I shot him a look. "I forgot, you knew the whole time."

"I did, and it angered me. But alas, I couldn't do anything about it without you realizing something was up. You were very good at covering your tracks when it came to him, even more so than when you were on missions for me. I just wished you put the same amount of effort you did for him when you worked for me."

"Just shut up," I growled.

"Oh no, are you getting angry at me? Are you going to lash out just like your family does when they are angry?"

I looked away, shaking my head. "No, I won't give you the pleasure."

I took a sip of my tea. It was not strong enough to calm me in this situation.

"I am impressed you actually betrayed Jack though. I never thought you had it in you. That is, if you aren't lying to us now and have been communicating with him this entire time. I wouldn't put it past you."

"I am not. I am finding this planet so I have enough power to get away from the likes of you then he and I can be happy for the rest of our lives."

The corner of his mouth lifted. "Oh, you think he will forgive you for this? You are cute."

"He will forgive me. He will understand."

"Or you will follow in your father's footsteps and have the person closest to you betray you."

"He won't."

"Sure, he won't."

I got up and left Joss sitting there in the mess room. I just couldn't stand it any longer. Jack wouldn't betray me, I knew that to be a fact.

Or at least, I hoped he wouldn't.

The argument made me wonder if I should communicate with him, just to make sure he will forgive me. We were so close now that it probably wouldn't have mattered. Just when I was about to decide, my father appeared in front of me in the corridor.

I jumped. "Oh, father. I didn't see you there."

"Is everything all right? You seem rather flustered."

I shook my head. "It's nothing. Just…" I debated telling him about the dream. "I just had a strange dream. That's all."

"Again? Did the ghosts come back?"

"No, I checked. Apparently, this is just a dream. Or one of those prophecy dreams you spoke of."

He studied me. "You shouldn't be able to have prophetic dreams after getting rid of those spirits. It is the spirits that grant us the gift of prophecy."

"Then I guess it was just a dream showing my fears."

"What was it about?" he asked.

I shook my head. "Nothing, apparently. If the spirits are gone, then it isn't anything to worry about. I am just eager to go back to Sanshli, that is all."

Father looked like he wanted to protest, but said nothing else about it. "We should arrive soon, probably within two hours. Go get some more rest in your room and I will come get you when we are ready for descent."

I nodded. "Yeah, that sounds good."

I went to my room and sat on my bed. If the ghosts caused prophecies, then I had nothing to worry about. There was no way I would kill Jack, and there is no way that the monster was real. It was just a fear I had along with the stress of having to be on this ship. I just couldn't wait to get off of it and learn the power my father told me about.

Nothing would go wrong. I wouldn't let it.

I still could debate on whether to talk to Jack. I wanted to make sure he forgave me for what I did, and that he would run away with me when the time came. I took a deep breath, knowing I would regret it.

But I just couldn't go another moment without talking to him.

Jack… I'm sorry.

Cadi! For the love of… Are you okay? Did they hurt you?

What? No… This was on my own. I am sorry I left, I'm sorry that things had to end this way.

Cadi, please, tell me where you are.

Just outside Sanshli.

Shit, Cadi. Where is Sanshli? Please, tell me the coordinates so I can come get you.

… I can't, Jack.

Why not? Please, just talk to me.

I want to, Jack, I really do. But I must finish this on my own. I will come for you, though, and we can be together forever.

We can be together forever if you just tell me where you are. Then we can fix all of this and go back to the way things were.

How do you know it will end like that though? How do you know if ending Nygard and finishing what my mother had started would actually end everything? Why can't helping him and learning from him be a way out?

Because he destroyed a whole planet, my love. You aren't him, you don't need that power.

And what do I need then? Because I have been told my entire life what I need to do and not do and for the first time I am making the choice.

But are you really? Or are you just doing what your father is telling you to do.

I didn't know how to respond. He was right, in a way. My father was the one who wanted to give me this power, he was the one who said we needed to go.

But it still was my decision, and it was the only decision I felt I had ever made. It's my decision, and you can't stop me.

Cadi, please.

I will come get you once it is all over. I love you, Jack.

I cut the communication with him and took a deep breath. Even though we were almost to the planet, I felt like this was going to be a long adventure that I just wanted to end.

Chapter 26

There it was—Sanshli.

The planet lay before us, like an emerald gem hanging in space. I had to admit, it was one of the most beautiful planets I had ever witnessed. I wasn't sure if that was because of the magic emanating from it, or if it was because it was a vast jungle with many lakes and rivers.

I just wished I could have seen it in all its glory. Although, I guess I was alive back then, I just don't remember it.

The ship didn't freak out like it did when we first came here. There was no weird barrier, or if there was, maybe my father was able to stop it from making our ship crash. Whatever the reason was, I was thankful. I didn't want to go through that again.

It took about four hours for us to initiate the landing

sequence and enter the atmosphere. I felt anxious the entire time and was glad I was working with Logan, who made sure I didn't make any mistakes as we piloted down onto the surface. I didn't expect that I would have made mistakes, but he seemed to always be shadowing me. I guess it was just part of his personality.

We landed at the coordinates my father gave us. It was outside the ruins we found the statue in the first time we came here. I was glad to be closer to it this time and not have to hike all the way through the forest again.

Especially after all those dreams I had experienced.

As we disembarked from the ship, backpacks ready, I watched as father took a big inhalation and let it out slowly. He turned to me.

"It's good to be home."

I wondered how he could still call it home when so much had happened to it. It wasn't like the planet it once was. No, it was all nature and creatures that I didn't want to come across again.

He turned away from the city and smiled. "We won't be going to the city this time. We are going to a different location—a place that I have kept secret all this time."

My eyes widened. Were we going to hike far then? Damn it…

I glanced over at Joss, who seemed as surprised as I was. Did he not know there was another location? Although father had mentioned it, I figured it was still in the city. I guess I was wrong.

We started out, away from the city, trekking through the deep jungle. I wondered how much of this forest overgrew after all the people and cities were destroyed. It was strange to think that even if the humans were gone, the planet would just keep living its life, making a new habitat, and the creatures would flourish. Taking a deep breath, I realized how humid it really was. The air smelt sweet, even if it was hard to breathe as there was so much moisture in the air. It wasn't like this the first time and I wondered if it was because it was a different season.

It didn't seem like there were many enormous creatures in the forest, or they just kept us alone. The only large creature we saw last time was Brayen, who was a Sanshlian. For all I knew there could be more massive cats, wolves, or even bears in these forests.

At least this time I knew how to use my powers.

We could hear, and see, however, lots of birds and bugs. So many bugs. I had slapped at least ten off of me in the hour we had been walking. They tickled as their little legs touched my skin. They were annoying, and to be honest, bugs were my least favorite pests to deal with, and that included Tim.

Father kept moving on, not stopping for even a break. Although we all had super strength, it would still be nice to take a little break. I thought about saying something, but I didn't want to take any crap from the rest of the group. So I remained quiet, and we kept on going.

The scenery hadn't changed all that much. I wished I could slow down a little to take in everything around me. The plants were so exotic and I wondered what it would have been like to have grown up on this planet and learn all about them. Did they use them for foods? For medicine? I had so many questions and I doubted that I would get the answers anytime soon.

Father had said he was part of a caravan. Was the jungle this thick when he was here all those centuries before? Or was it a lot more traversable? I imagined there were wagons involved, but I could have been wrong. Maybe they had to carry everything on their backs.

That would have sucked.

I looked back. It was impossible to see the city now, although I figured we lost sight of it a while back. It seemed strange that a vast structure masked by all these trees. Even the city itself was almost completely overtaken by nature now. Maybe I could use my powers to see what it once was like. To see what it was like before it was all destroyed.

I admitted to myself that seeing the desolation of this place and knowing the man who had committed the act was right in front of me was rather strange. Did everyone here deserve to be demolished? Or was what Joss had said really starting to bug me—how he was a monster that only very few decided to side with?

Was I the same kind of monster?

I hated how much this was tearing me up inside, and how my mind seemed to enjoy going back and forth about it over and over again. Why was this so complicated? Why was it so hard to figure out what was right or wrong?

And why did I have to choose?

I decided the best action was to do what was best for

me and what would help me survive. I just wanted to hide the rest of my years, and that wasn't so wrong, now was it? I wouldn't be hurting anyone, but doing what was best for me. Everything else threatened that goal, and I didn't want that. No, I had to go with my father, it was the only way.

At least, that was what I kept telling myself.

Nygard stopped at a small clearing and took off his backpack. "We will break here for lunch."

I collapsed on the ground, glad to have finally stopped. I felt exhausted, although I knew it was in my mind compared to my body. I could keep going if it weren't for my mind wandering, and the fact I really hated the company so we were all quiet, avoiding any conversation.

We ate our protein bar lunches that were a lot tastier than the ones I was used to. These, I believed, had fruit pieces which seemed to add a lot more of a flavor profile than the plain ones I had always eaten on missions. I wish I had known there were these flavors after all these years, as I did like enjoying my meal. It wasn't something I could experience often, but when I did it seemed to soothe my mind and able to think straight. Many people forget the importance of a meal and never realize that it helps reset the mind and body after a hard day of work, no matter what that work was.

I laid on my back and looked up at what little I could see of the sky. It was bright blue, the sun now straight above. It was midday here, and I wondered how much further we had to go. The temperature was perfect outside, just as it was last time I was here. The temperature out in the open was rather hot, but under these trees it felt nice. I watched as birds flew overhead, tweeting back and forth at one another.

This place really was paradise.

"Would I be able to go back to when this place was thriving?" I asked out of nowhere. In my head it was related, of course, but everyone seemed to look at me with surprise when I asked the question.

Father didn't look over to me, but kept his eyes down at his protein bar. "No, no matter what magic we use, we can't bring this planet back to what it was. It's impossible. The time on this planet is always a straight line and no matter if you travel into the past, it will always be the future here."

What he said was hard to think about. It made sense, though, since this place looked similar to when we came, and the fact that the beast was gone. It answered a few questions I had.

"So the time for this planet passes the same as we experience it. When we time travel, so does this planet."

"Precisely. You understand it a lot better than most."

Sort of. It still made my head hurt a little. "I can accept crazy, I am used to it now."

He laughed. "That is for sure."

"Wait." Logan interrupted. "You are telling me we've returned to the future, our present, even though we traveled here while in the past."

"Yes," father answered.

Logan shook his head. "I just want to go back to where

I was before all this happened. I did not sign up for this theoretical physics crap."

Jane hit him in the arm. She must have not liked him saying talking that way to Nygard.

He looked at her, surprised. "Well, it's true."

"Yes, but you didn't have to say it out loud."

I wondered what their relationship could have been like if they hadn't been dragged into this fiasco. I felt bad for them, as this was not what they signed up for. Then again, Joss had this planned all along. Maybe he knew they would be helpful with this scheme, or that he could just trust them somehow. If the plan goes through, they're benefiting somehow.

Especially with Tim. If I were him, I would have never trusted him. He has no control over his temper, and he always gets in trouble. I mean, usually I'm involved, but it still counted.

Nygard clapped his hands together. "Right, we should get going. We still have a bit farther to go for the day."

He made it sound as if we would be traveling the next day as well. I did not look forward to that at all.

As we started back through the jungle, I asked the question that I believed to be on everyone's mind. "Why didn't we just land closer to where we are going?"

Father smiled. "Because the city is the only place left with an area big enough for me to land on."

"Ah." I said, not wanting to press it any further. He knew the planet better than I did, so he must know all the spots in which he could land.

Tim gave me a smirk, as if I was stupid for asking the

question. I stuck my tongue out at him. I could not wait to be rid of him.

We walked for what felt like another four hours. I was curious if we were going to another town, or if the location of what we were looking for was something else entirely. I trusted my father knew the way, but as we kept on walking, I wondered if we were lost or not. This place had overgrown a lot, and since it was always going forward in time like us, it couldn't have even changed slightly since the last time I've been here.

But if it could do that, he would be prepared for it.

So the best option would be to wait it out and see where he would take us.

The sun seemed to be getting low in the sky and I hoped we would find a bigger area to stay for the night. The ground was very uneven here, and I didn't feel comfortable staying somewhere that I couldn't see far in the distance. Not to mention the fire could get out of hand and spark a wildfire or something. I mean, we had powers to stop that, but it still was a worry in the back of my mind, damaging any of the foliage here would not be a pretty sight.

I could see a clearing coming up and was excited that this would be our stopping point. Or at least I had hoped so. Watching my father, I could see his eyes shine a little. Yes, this was it.

We came out of the jungle to a massive lake. On the other side of the lake was a waterfall that came cascading down.

My mouth dropped. This was it—this was the place

from my dreams. Shit, was the creature real? Was this where we were all going to meet our end?

Father placed his hand on my shoulder and I jumped.

"What is it?"

I shook my head. "It's nothing. Sorry, I was just amazed by this scenery. It is a beautiful lake."

"That it is. We will stop here for the night, then in the morning we will arrive to our destination."

I nodded and started setting up camp with the others. Tim made a fire using his elemental fire magic. For once it came in handy. We all sat around the fire and ate our second helping of protein bars for the day. The fruit was no longer satisfying. I just wanted actual food.

"Emperor Nygard," Joss began. "We have done all you ask and followed you here. What is to become of us? I am certain you have a plan?"

It surprised me Joss came all this way without a detailed plan of what Nygard wanted. Then again, too many questions asked could make Nygard boot him and find someone else.

"I will reward you, don't you worry. Your family has served me for generations, and I will not forget that."

Joss bowed a little. "Thank you, sir. My generals here have also obeyed everything you have asked. Will they be given the same?"

Nygard nodded. "Of course. You all have served me well for this past year and a half. When we right this timeline and go back to the future, you all will be free to live how you please."

I wasn't sure if father was telling the truth, or if he was

telling them something they wanted to hear. He never specified to me we were going back to the future, or if he would go back to when he ruled and make sure his reign never ended. I never knew what he was thinking, and that frightened me a little.

As the fire died down and we also went to our tents to rest, I sat by the embers, watching as they smoldered away.

Something was bothering me. I could feel something here—an energy of sorts. Was it the creature from the dreams? Or was it something else?

Nygard sat down next to me, also watching as the fire dwindled. "Something on your mind?"

I shrugged. "I was just wondering what this place was. It has a lot of energy behind it, hidden away somewhere. I can't quite pinpoint it."

"You are growing stronger to sense the energy of this planet. I am glad you are more attuned to everything around you, it will make your training easier."

"How long will I need to train? I thought you said it was just a ceremony."

"There will be a ceremony for you to gain the power of immortality, yes, but you will still have to learn how to use your power, and how to make it so no one can take your life away."

I didn't know how to respond to that. Did I really want the power of immortality? I wanted forever, yes, but would Jack have the same? Or would I have to watch everyone die just as he had?

Was that a price worth paying?

Chapter 27

I woke to someone's hand over my mouth. I was ready
to slash whoever it was with the knife I had kept under
my pillow, something I normally did, when I realized it
was my father. After I calmed down, he lifted his hand.

"Come with me and bring your weapons." His face
was serious, more serious than I had ever seen him. I
wasn't sure what was going on, but my heart still felt as
if it would jump out of my chest. I took a few deep
breaths, trying to calm down.

I grabbed my weapons, which were all laid out and
ready to be used. I could never be too careful on
missions, or in general. I usually had at least three
weapons, if not more, near where I slept to use in case
anything happened in the middle of the night. I had been
ambushed before, and I knew in this line of work, it

would more than likely happen again.

Yay me.

I got out of my tent to find dawn barely breaking. None of the others seemed to be up, the only sounds coming from the birds in the jungle all around, starting to chant that it was morning. If I wasn't so distracted by what my father wanted, I would have appreciated the scenery.

Nygard motioned me to follow him and I did as he asked. He seemed to be trying to stay quiet, to not wake up the others, so I stayed quiet. Once we were far enough from the others, I would ask him the questions that were on my mind, but until then I knew it would be better to stay silent.

My mind wandered. Where was he taking me? Was it going to be like my dream where some creature would come out and try to take over my mind and spirit? Or were we going to leave the others and abandon them? I really hoped it was the latter as I had no attachments to any of them. Logan was the closest, and even then I didn't care.

We made our way up the steep hill and I knew we were no longer within earshot of the others. I could finally ask him what was going on. "Where are we going? Why did you wake me up?"

He smiled. "I am glad you trust me enough to wait this long to ask what we were doing. It makes me happy."

"I also know that you were trying to keep quiet around the others so I waited until they couldn't hear us."

"I see. I guess I could have told you I used a spell on them so they wouldn't wake up for at least another hour."

I sighed. "Yeah, you could have told me that."

"I will note that for next time."

"Why did you want to leave them behind? Why come all this way to just abandoned them?" I asked. To me, it made little sense.

"Because I don't trust them. I wasn't sure what was awaiting us here, not after you having all those dreams, so I decided to let them come most of the way to be our bodyguards. Now that we are close, I don't need them anymore."

So what he said to them earlier was a lie, he didn't intend to help them in the end, he was still just using them. I mean, I didn't blame him as they weren't the greatest people in the universe. But did they deserve how easily they were being tossed aside. Well, maybe Tim.

"Important lesson to learn, my daughter, is not to trust anyone, if they swear their allegiance to you. Will you remember that?

"I will."

"Now, about where we are going. We are going to where I trained all those years ago. The book in the capital was a fake. It's a complicated story for why that was, but they put it there to lead me out in the open. At the time, I didn't know it was a fake and hoped one of the other books had survived. The one I had is hidden behind this waterfall. Only I know where it is because you have to literally walk through rocks in order to find it."

That made sense since no other people besides Illusionists could find it, other than those who could control rock, but with it being behind a waterfall like that, it would be an ordeal to try to move the rock without destroying the landmark. As for the Illusionists, we would be able to walk through it. Once we knew how, that is.

I sort of knew how to go through rock, as I had hidden the gem in the trophy using that technique. I just had never used my entire body. It would just be a little more concentration, right?

"I do want to ask," father began as we kept up our ascension to the waterfall. "Was this the place you dreamed of? With the monster attacking?"

I nodded. "Yes, it was."

"Interesting. Since all the people you saw were ghosts who had lost to me in the war, they were able to figure out where my real book was. The only way they would have been able to do that was by being in the spirit world. Very fascinating.

"I presume the creature you saw was how they saw me and the evil things I did. Or, at least, what they thought was evil. I was merely protecting myself, and doing what I thought was right. It wasn't my fault that so many people disagreed with me."

I didn't say anything, as I still didn't know how I felt about everything, whether he was the hero or the villain of the tale. It was a lot more complicated than I wanted to get into. Saving one's own skin, though, seemed like the right thing to me. Then again, I had destroyed so many that had been in my path before. Maybe I was just making up excuses for the things I had done. My actions had mirrored his, maybe I was just the same kind of monster he was.

Maybe Joss was right.

"That would make sense," I said. "They would give your power a separate entity to scare me, and make me think you were some monstrous creature, possessed or something."

"Yes, their tactics seem a bit wreakless. I think they have figured out that you won't betray me or destroy me and have resorted to desperate measures. I am glad you don't fall for that sort of thing, though, as that would have been gravely disappointing."

Did that mean he had high expectations for me, or that if I had betrayed him for those reasons he would have killed me on the spot? I decided not to ask as I didn't want to know what the answer was.

As I followed my father up over to where the top of the waterfall was, I realized I could have been trained years ago if my mother hadn't hidden me from him. Would I have been the same person? Would I still have followed him like this, or since the war would have been fresher in my mind and I wouldn't have committed the terrible things I had done under Neil? Would I have still followed him like this?

It seemed like all my life now was asking questions and debating morality. I hated it. I just wanted to be free from all of this.

The sun was up by now and I could see the tops of the trees all the way back to the city we had landed near. It was a miraculous sight as birds flew over the treetops, dancing to the morning rays. I wished I could stay here forever and watch as the planet lived and breathed. It was beautiful.

And it had been destroyed because of one man.

We reached the top of the waterfall and I looked out. Now we were much higher than most of the trees and I could almost feel like I could reach up and touch the sun. I loved being up high. Maybe it had to do with Jack's office being near the top of the tallest building in Recar. Or maybe I just enjoyed having an authoritative spot.

"It's beautiful." I said as we both took a moment.

"It truly is. I always wanted to take your mother up here, but she refused to learn about the ways of our people. I am glad I can finally bring you here. Now," he turned to me and smiled. "We will sink down into the earth beneath us. Do you think you can do it?"

No.

"Yes." I responded, even though doubt poured into my mind.

He took a deep breath. "I can tell you aren't trusting yourself. Why is that?"

"Because it took me so long to just be able to place the gem inside that trophy. I don't know if I will be able to transfer my entire body into the ground."

"It is the same thing, you just have to trust yourself. Trust me, okay? Trust that I will hold your hand the entire time and you will be okay?"

I nodded. "Okay."

"Trust me and breathe, okay? Don't let fear overcome your desire to go into this place."

I took a deep breath, wondering if he meant fear of going through solid ground or fear of finding what was on the other side. Maybe it was both.

"Now." He said as I felt us sink into the ground.

This was most definitely harder than putting the gem in the trophy. He lied.

I could feel panic take over and it felt like I was being dragged through the dirt instead of gliding through like it should have been. I couldn't breathe, but I was too afraid to scream as dirt might enter my mouth and suffocate me.

This was pure torture.

My hand was still tight around my father's. Don't let go, I told myself. Don't let go.

I didn't want to die like this, yet the more we fell, the more it felt like that would be a possibility. This seemed endless—as if we would fall straight through the planet. Why was his hideout down here? Why couldn't it have been so much simpler?

Because I was never that lucky.

Moments passed and I finally gasped for air, which was a big mistake. Dirt filled my mouth and I couldn't do anything to get it out. I just had to wait it out until it was over and cough up all the debris.

It better be soon or I was going to die, I swore.

Suddenly we dropped down and were in a cave-like

area. I fell to the ground, coughing and spitting out all the dirt that had gotten into my mouth. I was finally on solid ground—no longer falling through the earth. I wanted to stay low to the ground, kissing it in thanks.

I didn't actually kiss the ground.

I did, however, take deep breaths, trying to regain my sanity. I did not want to do that again. How the heck were we going to get out of this area? Would we have to do it all over again? Why couldn't there be a better way?

Father bent down and patted my back. "You did well, daughter. You are as strong as I had hoped."

Was that some kind of test? Seeing if I would trust him, or to see if I would get through whatever barrier he had around this place?

When I was finally able to, I looked around. The cave was somehow lit, as if the lanterns in here had being giving off light for all of time. It was magic, I could tell, as I could feel it radiating through this place. The area was a lot larger than I thought, probably taking up the entire area beneath the lake. I wondered why we couldn't have just traveled starting from the side of the lake rather than from on top of the waterfall. Probably so he could see how much power I really had.

I wondered what would have happened if I didn't survive. Would he have saved me or would he have just let me die? Something told me I didn't want to know the truth.

There was a grand circular table that took up a big chuck of the area in front of me and Nygard, with chairs surrounding it. I wondered who all sat at the table or if it was a hope that Nygard had—believing that he would have comrades that would fight with him. On the other side of the entire cave was a small table with a book laid out.

That was the book he would use on me. It was the book that had all the spells an Illusionist like me could use.

So why was I so terrified?

"Are you ready, Myra? To become the most powerful being in this entire universe?" Nygard held out his hand to help me up.

Chapter 28

I lifted my hand. It was trembling harder than I have ever experienced. I didn't know what I wanted. Being powerful sounded great, but living forever... was that really what I wanted?

It was, I told myself. It had to be. Then I could be with Jack for as long as I ever wanted. This was the only way.

"I am ready."

He took me to the book. The binding was similar to the ones we had found to locate Sanshli the first time, however it was much larger and more worn. This book appeared as if it had been created at the beginning of time itself, yet somehow hadn't turned to dust. The pages were tattered and beige, with black and deep red ink dying each page. My father flipped through it with ease.

"All I wanted was to bring order back to this planet. The Illusionists used to rule this planet until the people could round up all the spell books and burn them. This is the only one that survived, at least to my knowledge. I found it just by chance in this place. An ancestor of mine, of yours, came to me in a dream and told me of its whereabouts. This was somewhere the high elders met, somewhere none of the other Sanshlians knowledge of, or could even get to.

"I trained here whenever I could and told no one else about it, not even your mother. She never got to see this place. No one did. I told them what I had found, and they all turned against me. I never understood why she…" he trailed off for a moment, then went on. "I had hoped we could spend all of eternity together, but I was wrong. Then she hid you from me and I searched everywhere for you. I don't know how she could put you in a different century, as she never trained with the book, but she somehow did. She could do a lot without that book, just using her intuition. She was strong and I wished she would have just understood."

He had risked everything when he told his people, and they didn't trust him. I wondered why he kept going, and why he thought I would be different.

"I knew if I found you, that you would understand. You are my blood, you know where I am coming from, I can feel it. You have your mother's intuition and my understanding of the world. Together we can rule the galaxy. Just as it should be."

That's when it hit me—why Nygard hadn't become

immortal. "You didn't want to become immortal until someone agreed to do it with you, did you?"

He paused, as if he was shocked that I said what was on his mind. His hand fell to his side as he looked over at the table. "I have waited so long for someone to come here with me and understand why I had done the things I did. The Illusionists in general have long life spans, and with my power I was nearly immortal. It was impossible to stop me and after this spell, I doubt anyone in the universe will be able to stop me—stop us."

All of this—everything he did was to bring me here. He didn't enjoy being alone like he was. I knew the feeling. However, he was the one who destroyed everything—he had caused his own loneliness.

But no one had sided with him. If I could remember those things that happened, if I had seen the horrors, would I still have stood here, wanting to be with him? Or would I have just run away?

I could sense his loneliness, and how he somewhat even regretted the things he did. He did it to bring back order, only to be treated as if he was the enemy. Even his own people turned. Would I have been able to forgive my people? Or would I have turned and done the same things as him?

Something told me I was just like him.

Watching father, he was still deep in thought, staring at the table he once believed his people would sit at and rule over Sanshli once again. But they betrayed him and believed he was evil. I didn't think he was, though. Power was safety. Power was making sure everyone

around you would be all right and not come to harm—
not to be oppressed.

"Should we begin?" I asked.

Father blinked a couple of times and came out of his
trance. "Yeah, let's begin."

Flipping through the pages, he found the spell he was
looking for. "This spell is rather long and very
complicated. You have to trust me fully, all right? It will
bring a lot of demons from your past up and I am sure
some of the ghosts of those who have died might try to
pull something into our vulnerable state. Make sure you
stay brave, daughter."

The way he was talking made me fear what it all
would entail. Was this not a spell the Illusionists did? Or
was it one that was forbidden even by the Illusionists of
old?

Then it occurred to me—if this gave an Illusionist
immortality, then wouldn't the older Illusionists still be
alive?

"Father, what happened to the others who have used
this spell? Why are there not more like us?"

Father hesitated for a moment, as if he didn't want to
answer. "I… I don't think many survived the ceremony,
and those who did I think were slaughtered by the other
Sanshlians before they finished the ceremony. In fact, I
think it was why our people had been outcastes and all
the books burned. This was the last and most powerful
spell they ever created." He turned to me with a smile.
"But we will survive, Myra, you are powerful enough. I
know we are."

He may have been, but I really doubted that I was.

"How do you know I am powerful enough? I barely made it through that rock, and that was a simple spell for a Sanshlian. Maybe we should wait—"

"No! I have waited long enough! We must do this before time runs out!"

Time runs out? Was there something he wasn't telling me? We were in some kind of danger? Or was his lifespan coming to an end?

"What aren't you telling me, father?" I asked. "What time is running out?"

I took a deep breath. "My life. The sword that had frozen me in time, I can feel that time slowly coming back to me and I am afraid I might not have much longer. Without this immortality spell, I will cease to exist. But I do not want to do it alone—I do not want to be the only Illusionist left. That is why I am glad you were the one who found me, and so we can finally fulfill this prophecy and take the galaxy to a new era that should have existed a long time ago."

But was that what I wanted? I just wanted to be with Jack—to hide somewhere and forget everything that had happened. Would performing this spell really do that? Or would it bring more trouble than it was worth?

And would I never die? Or would I just never die of old age? There were still so many questions that hadn't been answered. I wanted more time to think about it, but by the sound of it, my father didn't have time.

This was the only way to save him—but was he worth saving?

"Fine," I said. "We will perform this ceremony. What do I need to do?"

Father went through the steps, explaining a drop of my blood was needed, then we would go into a deep meditation to face all the demons of our past. Once that was done, and we succeeded in those trials, we would be offered immortality. It seemed easy enough, except that the demons of both of our pasts were pretty big. Did he really think he could face his? Could I face mine?

I guess there was only one way to find out.

Father took a knife and pierced the tip of my finger, dropping it into incense he already had burning.

"Repeat these words: 'fiar ravat kabal nho sanshi travas'."

Here goes nothing. "Fiar ravat kabal nho sanshi travas."

It was like I was being sucked into a different world. Everything was black and I couldn't see any which way.

"Father?" I called out. "Are you there?"

There was no response. I was utterly alone. I tried to look around, but I couldn't see anything. It was cold, dark, and I didn't know what I could do.

Suddenly a light appeared, and I ran straight to it, believing it to be my only escape.

I wish I had stayed in the dark.

The scene I came across was one that I never wanted to face again—it was the scene of my adopted father's death.

I remembered the scene like it was yesterday. The Empire had landed on our planet, looking for P.A.E.

sympathizers and had butchered all of them. My adopted father, Ben Archer, was one of them.

We were supposed to escape and find our uncle and he would take us somewhere safe. It was supposed to be all of us, including father.

But that wasn't what happened.

Bullets rained down through the orchard as father and I ran together. Rik had run way ahead as he was always faster than I. Father probably stayed with me to make sure I was safe.

It was my fault he was shot. If I had only been stronger and faster, I could have gotten out of there and he would still be okay.

I watched as he fell to the ground, blood soaking his once clean shirt.

This wasn't happening. No, it was just a memory. I wasn't really here.

"Please promise me you will remember everything I have taught you," my father called out to me. "Find Rik and go with the others and live your life, Arcadia. Do what is right."

Tears streamed down my face. My father had one request of me and I failed him. I didn't live the way he wanted me to live—I lived my life in a selfish way, killing those who were in my way.

I was a monster.

I watched my younger self run off towards Rik, knowing I would never make it—knowing the only thing that awaited me were the Kamps.

The place that would change my life forever.

A place where I had to kill or be killed.

The scene changed and I found myself a couple of years older, injected with so many different experimental meds, hair shaven close to the scalp, and given a barcode. We were never called by a name, but the number given to us. I will never forget, I was 1318KXT.

I couldn't move as I watched my younger self kill other children—children who had been kidnapped and forced into the same situation I was. We had to do it, or we would have been killed.

This wasn't fair—they weren't choices I made, but choices that were made for me. If I didn't do what was ordered of me, then I would have died long ago.

I did everything so precisely so I could get close to the Emperor. The drugs they gave me were supposed to make me follow orders, and I acted the part. I acted as if I couldn't disobey any order given to me no matter how hard I tried so that the scientist could present me to the Emperor and I could murder him for everything he had done. And I tried, but failed, only to be given an offer of survival.

So I took it.

At first, I had tried to kill the Emperor so many times, but he could survive each of my attempts. I wasn't sure how at the time, but now I knew he was reading my mind.

He was using me to get to Sanshli.

The area faded and I was shown a scene I didn't want to relive—even more so than my adopted father dying.

The time when I killed my own uncle.

I knew it was him, I remembered as a kid, he was John Basen, the man who taught my brother and I about plants and animals, the uncle Rik and I had gone camping with, explored so much of Garvner with.

The uncle that stood in my way during a mission—the uncle that sacrificed himself so that the leaders of the P.A.E. I was supposed to kill could get away unscathed.

It was then I realized that the leaders I were supposed to kill must have been Rik this entire time. What would have happened if my uncle hadn't intervened? Would I have killed my own brother? Part of me wanted to say no, but the other part of me was watching as I stabbed my own uncle in the heart.

I would have killed my brother that day, there was no doubt in my mind.

"Your father would have been so disappointed in you." Those were the words he whispered in my ear—words that caused me to falter and start rethinking my entire life.

Everything went dark again. I glanced around, looking for a way out, but there was nothing. All I could hear were my own thoughts.

My cheeks were still wet from crying. What had I done with my life? Why didn't I take that moment right there to join my uncle and help him? Why did I no longer think it was right? Was it because of the magic Neil was using on me? No, it didn't feel like it—it felt like my own decision. How could I do that? How could I hurt my own family, one of the people who raised me?

Why did I become so cold?

He was right, my adopted father would have been disappointed. I would have been one of the people he wanted destroyed in the galaxy. I wasn't fighting for others, willing to risk my life for the common good. I was doing everything to save my own skin, a selfish act that drove me to hurt those who had done nothing but help me in my past.

And that included Jack.

He had done so much for me and I had betrayed him too. Would I end up killing him? Would everything have been for nothing? Would I just be like my father—my real father—and destroy his life too?

Was I the same monster that could never atone for the things she had done?

I collapsed down and hugged my knees. I didn't deserve immortality. I was something that should be destroyed. Someone who was good should have immortality, not me. I deserved death.

As I thought that, I could feel all the spirits that still inhabited this world come forth. They saw I was weak and they were ready to pounce. They encircled me, whispers in the language of old.

"Pierf!"

I closed my eyes, ready for the last strike. This would be how it all ended—this was what I deserved.

"Jack… I'm sorry."

Then there was an explosion and I was back in the room father had brought me to. He stood in front of me, his arms up, using his magic to block the explosion of rock and water that was now heading towards us.

What the heck had happened?

It appeared as if Nygard was using all his strength to move the rock away from us, throwing it back into the jungle, not afraid of what it might destroy. As I looked up at the now clear sky above us, I saw what had happened.

There was a ship hovering above us.

"Jack?" I whispered.

Father lifted his arms again and I watched as the ship faltered. I jumped up.

"Father, no!" I screamed. I knew Jack was on the ship and I did not want to see him perish. Not like this.

"They will be fine, one of them can control metal. We just need them out of the sky and at a better advantage."

With that, the ship crashed into the ground. He was right, though; the ship didn't become as damaged as it should have. Alan had been keeping it safe.

So Jack and the others were able to follow us. I didn't even begin to understand how that was possible.

"Looks like we have some guests. I was hoping we could have done the spell without this trouble, but I guess I was wrong. Are you ready to fight, daughter?"

I watched as my brother and the others started coming out of the ship, ready to fight. I glanced over and saw that Joss and his team were on the other side of the room, preparing as well. "That depends, which ones are our enemy?"

"Any who get in our way."

That was a simple enough answer. I didn't care for any of them except for Jack, who I didn't believe could get in my way.

"Stay with the spell book and protect it. I will take care of the rest. Don't worry, Myra, nothing will happen to you as long as I am here."

He started to go forward when I grabbed his sleeve. "Wait, don't hurt Jack. He won't betray me."

Nygard studied me for a moment, then nodded. "Fine. I promise to keep him safe. But if he does anything to hurt you, I can't guarantee his safety."

"He won't hurt me." I repeated.

Father didn't say a word as he turned to the others and flew up in the air.

This would be the battle to end all battles, and it would decide the galaxy's fate.

Chapter 29

This battle was more chaotic than any I had witnessed in my entire life.

I mean, I usually worked alone in the shadows anyway, so I didn't get to see much of the enormous battles, but I had seen some. Seeing people who could all use magical powers one way or another go at it, however, was much more impressive.

And if it weren't for the fact that this would probably be a battle to the death, it would have been really spectacular.

My brother, of course, was the first to attack, using the earth elemental magic to bring two large columns up to try to smash Nygard. It was a pathetic attack, to say the least, as Nygard punched them and it all went crumbling down.

Tim and Logan went straight towards my brother and the others, Tim's hands were bursting with flame already. He finally got to use them for an all-out fight and I had a feeling he was excited about that. Logan was already summoning ice and throwing it straight at Alan and Lance. Alan was able to fling a piece of metal at them to slow them down a bit, but it wasn't enough. As Alan distracted them more and more, Lance made a run for it towards Joss.

And I just stood there, feeling like a useless idiot.

Father had said to stay back with the book, and I knew if I left someone would try to make a break for it to destroy it. I mean, this was all it was about, right? The power of this book? My brother wanted it destroyed, Joss wanted to use it to gain more power, although I wasn't sure how that was possible, and father wanted it to gain immortality.

All of this chaos was because of this book.

I glanced over at it, making sure I could still see the battle in the corner of my eye. It was because of this book that the people of this planet were destroyed. It wasn't Nygard that was the source of all the wars and pain and chaos. It was this book.

So what should I do?

If I destroyed it, I knew my father would kill me in an instant, then probably regret it right after. He would still be powerful though and be able to bring back his version of the galaxy. Then again, he said all those years were slowly catching up to him and he believed that he would not live much longer. So would it be a good idea to destroy this book?

Or should I try again to gain immortality and stop all this chaos?

I could feel the book beckoning to me, its energy and power emanating off of it like heat from lava. I had a feeling if I even tried to destroy the book, it would protect itself. It was sentient.

Was it the creature I had dreamt about?

Without warning, a giant piece of metal came straight towards my face—its sharp point threatening to skewer my skull. I raised up my hand in a shield and it quickly bounced off.

That was a close one. I needed to pay more attention to the battle and decide what I would do with the book later.

I glanced around to find Jack nowhere to be seen. Where did he go? I knew he had to be with the others, I could sense him. I thought about trying to communicate with him, but I knew that could distract him if he was battling someone and I didn't want to be the cause of his death. No, I would have to just wait it out.

My father raised his hands, and black clouds formed in the sky. The sound of the thunder roared above, and I knew exactly what he was going to do.

He was going to summon and control the lightning.

It appeared as if everyone around also knew what he was going to do and quickly took cover, running either into the jungle or under the ship.

The light was blinding as Nygard took control of it and sent it straight into the ship. I watched as the ship exploded, pieces flying in every direction. I quickly put my shield back up around me and the book to protect us from the shards. It was amazing to see such power.

I wanted that power.

I shook my head. Was that me or the book talking? I glanced over at it, unsure of the source. The closer I stood to it, the more I noticed my desire for power rose.

Maybe it wasn't because of the Illusionists that these books were destroyed, but because they became a power in and of themselves.

There wasn't time to think about it as I saw a figure running this way. It was Joss and Jane.

I wasn't sure what they wanted and kept the shield up. With all this chaos, I wouldn't have put it past Joss to try to take control. It would make perfect sense, especially after everything he had put me through.

"Myra," Joss said as he approached. "Grab the book and let's get out of here. If we hide in the jungle, your father will get rid of the Republic without having to worry about you and the book. Then we can meet up with him afterwards. Lower your shield."

What he said made sense, but I shook my head. "No, he would have told me that was the plan. I am just going to wait here."

"You are going to get hurt. Come with us."

"You have never cared whether I got hurt before. I think you are trying to trick me."

"Stop being difficult and come on!"

"No!" I yelled out.

Joss let out a breath. "Fine, Jane! Now!"

I was right, they were trying to get me to lower my defenses to get to the book.

Jane tried to use her power of controlling plants against me, with vines coming straight at me like daggers, but with my shield, it was useless. They also must not have paid attention to the races, as father wasn't the only one who could control this storm.

I raised my hand and summoned the forces of nature and demanded a bold of lightning come crashing down upon them. Light burst and energy burst through the room. The chairs and table exploded into hundreds of pieces.

And Joss and Jane were no more.

I couldn't believe what I had just done. I had killed them.

Logan was the first to notice and screamed out for his love. Ice shards came raining upon me, but none could break through my shield.

But I knew he wasn't going to give up.

"I'm sorry, Logan," I whispered as I raised my hand. With another bolt of lightning, he was gone.

I had to protect this book at all costs, and I couldn't let anyone stand in my way.

It felt like a little thread of darkness was weaving into my heart.

"Pierf."

I tried to listen to the voice coming from the book. It wasn't like the ghost voices from before, but was something completely different. This was the book itself.

And it felt alluring.

I touched the soft, tattered pages, the voices getting stronger. Were these the Illusionists from before? Or was it something completely different? All I knew was that I wanted more of whatever power it was giving off.

I could understand what my father saw in it, and why he was mad at the rest of the planet. They had tried to take away this power and destroy it. They were the ones who were monsters—they had destroyed an entire culture out of fear.

This power wasn't bad. It could be used for good. There was no reason to fear it.

I couldn't push away the thoughts anymore—it wanted me. It needed me. And I needed it. I needed this power.

I couldn't finish the immortality spell, as my father was doing it with me, but there were so many spells I could use right now—ones that would stop all the people against me. I could end those who were trying to stop me once and for all.

Flipping through the pages, I found spells upon spells that I could use to stop anyone—ones that would lock them in stone for an eternity, and ones that would destroy them in a way that they would never come back again, even with the use of magic. There were so many choices.

And all of them felt intoxicating.

I stopped, shaking my head, trying to get this thing out of my head. It was trying to pull me in—it wanted to consume me. I wouldn't let it. I was more powerful than this book thought I was.

Although I needed to protect it, I backed away. I had to distance myself so I couldn't feel the energy pulsating from it. I used my magic to make a barrier, however, so that no one could touch me or the book. I focused on that as I watched the battle ensue.

Father was still battling my brother and Alan. They didn't have a chance as my father brought down lightning strike upon lightning strike on them. The only reason they had survived this far was because of my brother's power that enabled him to control the earth. He was able to block each and every strike by making a shield over himself and the others.

I still didn't see Jack. Was he all right? Was he just hiding? Or had he gotten hurt when the ship crashed?

I wanted to check in with him through our connection, but I also didn't want to distract him when he could have been fighting. Glancing around, I also couldn't see Tim.

Great, he would probably pop out of nowhere and try to kill me.

I had the shield up so he wouldn't be able to do it as easily as he thought he could. For all I knew, Tim could have died battling my father, as I didn't see his flames anywhere. He excelled in making an entrance.

That's when I heard something smack into my shield behind me. I turned to find Tim rubbing his face. I gave him a smirk.

"Did you really think I would be that careless?" I asked.

His hand flamed up. "I had hoped. But alas, it seems I have underestimated you again. Now lower this shield so we can fight it out once and for all."

"Nope."

His face started to turn red like his hands. "Come on, Myra, we can finally decide this once and for all—to the death."

I shook my head. "No, I don't really care to fight you, especially since I have nothing to prove. I already know I am stronger than you."

"Oh yeah? Then show me!"

That's when a bullet went straight through his head and bounced off my shield. Tim slumped down onto his knees and fell face-first onto the ground. Standing behind him was Jack.

"Satisfied?" I asked. I knew he had been wanting to kill him for quite a while now.

"Very."

I lowered my shield and went straight into his arms. "Jack, I'm so sorry. I didn't want to leave you, but I just didn't want my brother—"

He rubbed my back, keeping me close. "Shh, it's okay. You don't need to explain. Everything will be okay now. I promise."

I felt safe in his arms, not wanting to leave him ever again. "We can finally be together forever, Jack. You and I can escape all of this and have no one chasing after us. Then we can live our lives."

"That's all I want, Cadi. Just you and me."

He stroked my hair. "I'll protect you from everything. I will make sure that most of all, you stay safe."

Tears fell down from my eyes. "You are always there

for me, Jack, even though I left you behind. I don't understand."

He kissed my forehead. "I understand you, Cadi. I understand everything that is going on. She told me where to find you."

"She?"

I looked up at Jack, whose eyes were red with tears.

"I'm sorry, Cadi, but this is the only way to stop him and protect you in the future." With that, Jack stabbed me straight in the heart.

Everything after happened so fast—Jack laying me down on the ground. A great explosion shattered the entire area as my father screamed my name.

Then everything went white.

Chapter 30

I opened my eyes to find myself lying on a bed in the middle of a bleak gray room. My body was sweating, as I swore I was just dying a moment ago. I glanced around, trying to remember where I was and who I was.

I was Arcadia Archer, daughter of Ben Archer. I had just turned eighteen. I rubbed my forehead, trying to figure out what was going on. Father said to celebrate that he would bring me to Valle to one of the banquets. I was his guest.

Wait... Father was alive?

What was going on? Why did I have more than one memory of my past? I remember my father dying as we were hunted down by Imperials, but I also remember growing up on Garvner my entire life, with my father and my brother... and my mother Marissa. She wasn't dead, none of them had died.

What…

Uncle John Basen was still alive as well. I never killed him. Or did I? He adopted two boys and came to live on Garvner. I grew up with David and Will Basen. We were close; they were like my brothers. So what was this feeling I had? What were these memories that kept coming?

They didn't feel real—it felt as if I had woken up from a long dream that spanned my whole life. The memories were fuzzy, and correlated with a lot of what had happened, but everything was dark and I wasn't like that. I wasn't a cold-hearted killer. Or was I?

Sanshli… I remembered hearing stories when I was little about how the planet existed and one man destroyed the entire planet, but that was it. There was no story about taking the knife out of his statue in order to change the past.

Unless… that was exactly what happened.

I got up and ran into the bathroom. I had my dark brown hair and dark eyes. I was no longer blonde with violet eyes. I looked down at my wrist. There was no barcode. So was that all just a dream? Or was this the end of the spell?

I tried to remember what had happened. We were all on Sanshli and there was an enormous battle. Nygard was defeating everyone when… Jack stabbed me.

"Why did he stab me…" I whispered as tears fell down my cheeks.

Suddenly a figure appeared in the mirror. "Because I

told him to."

I screamed. I turned, but no one else was in the bathroom with me. I turned back to the woman, her violet eyes reminding me who she was.

"Violet… mother… no, all that couldn't have been real. There is no way."

She laughed. "It was. And thanks to your boyfriend, you were able to defeat Nygard."

I shook my head. "No, he was never defeated. I was killed."

"Nygard gave his life energy so you would live. It was the only way to defeat him—to make him have to give up his own life," she paused. "I'm sorry to have had to kill you to do it, but it was the only way."

My father… my real father was dead. He had given his life to me. "But… how? How am I back here?"

"With the last of his energy, and mine that was still around, he created the world where you wanted to live. He changed the past, and the future, so you would be happy. You are mortal now, with no powers, and returned to the life you wanted to live. And with the last of my energy, I was able to give you this message, and to tell you what really happened."

I couldn't believe what I was hearing—what had all transpired. As I looked in the mirror, I saw Violet start to disappear. "No, wait, I want to know more—"

"I'm sorry, Myra, but this is just a ghost form that can't last much longer. I love you, my sweet child, don't you ever forget that. We both loved you."

Tears ran down my face as I watched her disappear for

the last time. I collapsed on the floor, not understanding what had happened. I wasn't... human. I was a Sanshlian. All that had happened and this life that I lived now was just because my father had given all his power and energy to me.

The door to my room slid open and my father—my human adopted father—stepped in. "Arcadia, I heard you scream. What happened?"

I looked up at him, my eyes full of tears. "Father, tell me truth, what am I?"

He studied me for a moment, then sighed. "I take it you remember?"

I nodded, not expecting him to have known.

"Come sit on the couch with me and I will tell you what I know."

I followed him out into the living quarters. I glanced out the window to find that I was on Valle, the capital of the Second Republic. It hadn't fallen like it did last time.

"You were brought to us when you were just a couple of years old by your mother and father. When I saw them, I could tell something was odd, as if they weren't there. It was in fact just their ghosts. They were from Sanshli, as you know. They explained that one day you would wake up with memories of a past that would have happened. There was something about time travel and all that, but I didn't quite understand. I didn't believe them at first, but your mother did. She understood for some strange reason. We had always wanted a daughter and you were always special to us, and you still are. But other than them telling me about the time travel and that you would awaken to different memories of both timelines, they didn't say much more."

That made sense. He wouldn't understand the rest, and he might not have loved me if he knew what kind of killer I was. I took a deep breath.

"If you ever want to talk, Cadi, I'm here."

I smiled. "No, it is fine. It's too complicated to ever explain to someone."

"I still don't know why you had to remember instead of it always hidden away in your memories. I wish I could have stopped them from coming back."

I shook my head. "No, I needed to know what had happened. I like knowing where I came from, and what I was. You and mother will always be my parents—the ones who raised me. But knowing how I came to exist in this world... Understanding that has explained a lot of the things I have felt."

Father wrapped his arms around me. "I'm sorry we lied to you."

"I understand, and I probably wouldn't have believed you if you had told me, anyway. It's pretty farfetched, even with these memories. I'm not even sure if I actually believe it, and that this isn't the dream."

Father placed his hand on my shoulder. "Well, take your time to get ready. If you recall, I told you I would take you out to find yourself a dress for tonight."

Right, tonight was the ball for all the representatives. My father was a representative of Garvner. I had been excited for my first ball, but a little part of me dreaded going now. "Okay."

With that, he left me to sit there and ponder what would be my next plan of action. I wasn't the woman I used to be—I was no longer a killer. This world's version of me would never even contemplate hurting someone. Yet now…. There was so much blood on my hands.

That isn't me. I'm not a killer.

But the fact was that if pushed, I would have been. Wouldn't everyone? It was a lot to take in, and I knew it would be awhile before it really all sunk in. With a sigh, I went into the kitchenette and made myself some cherry tea.

At least that had stayed the same.

I felt like I was my father's shadow, which was very ironic. I simply followed him around while he talked to all the representatives and I stayed quiet. At least he let me have some champagne since I was old enough. I fiddled with my emerald dress, one that didn't show a bunch of leg like all the other dresses I had to wear in the past. It was spaghetti strapped with light ruffles made of satin that went down to my ankle. I still wore strapped heels since it would go best with the dress. They were white and complemented my clutch purse.

It was strange seeing some of the same people I had seen when this was the Imperial ball. Some representatives were still the same which showed that sometimes things are just meant to be. Although the officers and generals who were here were not the same, as Neil had picked young people to help him in his battle to find Sanshli. However, there was one person I spotted with his general father, and that was Tom.

I smiled a little as he stood in the back, leaning against the wall. He looked like he did not want to be there. At least this time I wouldn't have to hear his comments in my ear. I kind of wanted to talk to him and see what he was like to people he didn't know, or have a grudge against. I made a mental note to do that later. I wondered if I could still beat him in hand-to-hand combat. How would I even go about finding that out?

As my attention was elsewhere, father had begun to talk to someone else. As the person spoke, I whipped my head back around to find the person I didn't ever think I would see again.

"Jack!" I yelled as I quickly set my drink down and wrapped my arms around him.

"Arcadia, what do you think you are doing?" Father yelled as he pulled me back.

Jack laughed. "Friendly daughter you have there, Mr. Archer. Maybe I should visit your planet sometime, especially if all the women are just as friendly."

I glanced at father who was beet red. I studied Jack. He had the normal cocky grin, but it was different. He didn't look at me like he normally did. And he had two women wearing short dresses in tow. This was an unwelcome surprise.

Right... We have never met before. He doesn't know who I am.

"I... I'm sorry, Mister McHannon. I had mistaken you for someone else. Will you please excuse me?"

Before he could answer, I hurried towards the glass doors that led out onto the balcony outside. I had to get out of there before he saw the tears that were forming in my eyes.

Shit. I didn't think it would hurt this bad. I leaned out over the balcony, looking down at the city below.

Shit. Shit. Shit.

He didn't remember me. We wouldn't be together forever like we had promised. After everything we had gone through, he doesn't remember a damned thing. There were so many things I wanted to tell him, but he would just think I was crazy. I wouldn't blame him either. If someone said these things out of nowhere to me, I wouldn't believe them.

"Arcadia, what are you doing out here?" Father stepped out on the balcony.

I turned to him and forced myself to smile. "Nothing. Don't worry about me."

He sighed. "It has something to do with the memories, doesn't it?"

I gave up my smile and nodded.

"Look, I don't know what happened, but that man is bad news, Arcadia. He could have been the best prince to you in the past, but now he is just a player. He would just use you and get rid of you. I can't even count on two hands how many girls I have seen him with at these events. It is disgusting and I would never let you be with such a man."

I didn't know if that made me feel better or not. I had a father looking out for me now, but if I was honest, Jack hadn't changed at all. He was the same old Jack that I had always known, but I wouldn't tell my father that. I would just let him believe I wouldn't fall for someone like that. "Thank you, father. I just need a minute. Today was a lot to take in."

He nodded and left me out on the balcony. I looked back down at the city and sighed. What was next for me? I knew David in this life still had a thing for me, but I didn't feel the same for him, or at least not anymore. There could have been something there if I didn't remember the past. Now I just wasn't sure.

"Mind if I join you?" I heard a voice ask behind me. I turned to find Jack, smiling, standing by himself.

I felt myself blush. Now that I knew he didn't remember, I felt really embarrassed I had hugged him like that. "No, not at all. It's a free planet." In this timeline, at least.

"Thanks." He leaned against the balcony next to me. "Beautiful city, isn't it?"

I shrugged. "I guess. I like Anosira better. And Rec—" I paused, realizing what I had said.

He raised an eyebrow. "Recar? So you have been to my planet?"

I shook my head. "No, I had just seen it in some photos."

"And the friend you thought I looked like?"

I sighed. "It's complicated, and you wouldn't believe me anyway."

"I have heard some very crazy things in my lifetime, so try me."

I studied his eyes. They looked curious, as Jack did always like a good story. Seeing him standing there like this brought a smile to my face, and even now I felt I could tell him anything. "It involves Sanshli, and time travel, and super powers."

"Ah, so you are good at writing fables I see."

I rolled my eyes. "See, I knew you wouldn't remember."

"Remember?" He asked. "So I'm a part of this tale. I do hope I get all the girls, and fame of course."

I laughed. "Actually, you kind of do."

He did his famous half grin. "Well, maybe I will listen to your story then."

I paused for a moment, then shook my head. "No, it's a story everyone has forgotten. I will just let it go, like I should."

"That's a shame, I think every story should be shared with at least one person."

I smiled for a moment, then did the most outrageous thing I had ever done—I grabbed him by the collar and kissed him. Even Jack was surprised.

"And that, Mister McHannon, is as much of the story as I will tell you."

With that, I turned to leave when I felt him grab my wrist. I turned to face him, thinking I would find him wanting more, or something very Jack-like. Instead, I saw confusion and almost sadness on his face.

"Ca... Cadi..."

He remembered.

He pulled me closer and wrapped his arms around

me. "Cadi. I'm so sorry. I didn't know what… Violet told me… I am so very sorry."

I wrapped my arms around him. "It's all right Jack, everything is all right now."

"I remember everything. We can start over in this life." He leaned back to face me and smiled, his eyes still full of tears. "We can have a happily ever after."

With that, he kissed me strongly, pulling me close. In the corner of my eye, I could see my father running out towards the balcony. His face was red and he looked like he was about to start shouting.

Maybe things did always end up how they should.

Thank you so much for reading!

Readers like you make it possible for authors like me to write stories! If you could spare a moment and leave a review on Amazon, Goodreads, BookBub, and wherever you like to buy books, that would mean the world to me! It really helps authors like me to succeed in the publishing world.

A big thank you again for your patronage. I hope you will check out my other series I have published, and stay connected to learn about my many stories to come. Keep reading to get a sneak peak of one of my favorite series, Daughter of Hades: Endangered!

CHAPTER 1

Chrys

Hello and welcome to the Underworld. My name is Chrys, and I am the daughter of Hades. May I take your coat?

I really wanted to say that to the group of recently deceased that stepped up to my father, begging him not to send them to Tartarus, the place of eternal torment—pretty much where all the bad people went. Beside Father was Minos, Rhadamanthys, and Aiakos, the other judges of the dead. I sure as Cronus didn't want to be judged by that deadly trio. First off, they had been here longer than I had, since Zeus appointed them, and although nothing really ages here after death, they seemed to be older and grumpier than ever before. And I, unfortunately, had to witness today's session of pleas because "I needed to learn the ins and outs of the business in case anything ever happened." At least, that is what my father, Hades, kept telling me.

Father sat there, quiet, as the three stooges (that's what I called them in my head, if they ever found out, I would be in so much trouble) examined the next contestant. The man before them was on the fence of being sent to either Tartarus or the Asphodel Meadows, which was why he was being judged. I already knew my father's decision, since he was quite predictable when it came to judging people.

It would be Tartarus.

Father always took a long while, as if his decision hadn't already been made. He could have finished judging today's deceased already if he didn't take his time about it. It annoyed me tremendously, which I knew he could tell as I sat there nervously fighting with my dress sleeves.

One of the men went down on his knees. "Please, have mercy on me. I never meant to do those things, had I known— "

"Had you known, you would have been perfect, right?" Hades interrupted with a scowl. "Done everything you could to be in paradise? There are no second chances here, the gods have given humans a chance to obey them, a chance to live in paradise. It is not our fault you don't see the signs."

I let out a brief yawn, trying to cover it with my hand, but my father noticed right away and gave me one of his cold looks. I tried my hardest to sit up straight, to appear as though my mind hadn't drifted off to thinking about meeting up with my friends Huntley and A.J., or what I told Father was "being tutored about modern Earth affairs" by these friends of mine. Really, we just hung out and tried not to get into trouble.

Tried was the key word there.

"Tartarus. Send in the next one," Hades ordered.

Loud barking echoed through the throne room. I smiled as Cerberus came galloping towards the dead human. He screamed in terror as everyone did when greeting Cerberus. No one saw how clumsy this puppy really was, but thought it as one of the most terrifying beasts in all the Underworld. But I guess if he was taking me to my horrible fate, I would fear him too.

Nah, he's not scary. He's adorable.

The man screamed again as all three jaws bit at his clothes, dragging him out the door and down the chute that would send him to Tartarus. His soul would circle there in the deepest part of nothing for all of eternity.

Yawn. When would this be over?

I knew nothing else besides this life, as I have never traveled to any of the other worlds. A big complicated mess, but irritating nonetheless. Which led to why my friends and I got into just a bit of trouble every once in a while. But only in the Underworld, mind you. We couldn't ever leave.

My father judged different humans, demigods, and creatures for another hour. I tried not to let my stomach grumble, as that wasn't something the goddess of the Underworld should never let happen. I wasn't to show any weakness, I wasn't to show anything less than divine perfection.

Well, at least Mother wasn't back yet to make

matters worse.

Cerberus dragged away his last victim for the day while Father clapped his hands together. "Well that wraps up today. The three of you are dismissed. Chrys, come with me."

I felt as if my heart stopped, which would have been pointless even if it did because I was already in the world of the dead. So dying wouldn't get me out of the conversation I was dreading—the conversation of how I would eventually become goddess of all this. Boy, was I looking forward to that day.

It was way too much responsibility if you asked me. I just wanted to be a normal teen, even though I had been a teen for quite some time. The years passed by differently for the gods, something humans could never understand. And since I never really got to do what most teens did in any other world, I felt like I would never grow up and learn about the rest of the universe. I just wanted to explore, be able to go out into the worlds.

To be known.

"Yes, Father." I followed after him as he headed towards the hallway. Knowing Father, he was going to the patio that looked out at his entire world for a "talk." He was so predictable, especially after all this time. When you have Hades as your father, and he was the only constant in your life, you're bound to know him more than you want to, and spend more time than needed in the drab Underworld.

I was a few steps behind him, watching as he had his hands folded neatly behind himself, his short hair nicely trimmed, a new style the mortals were sporting. I didn't blame him for wanting to try to fit in with those that had recently died. That way they felt more at home. Except those who went to Tartarus. He didn't really care to fit in with those souls.

Cerberus sat in his corner of the hallway, next to the patio door, gnawing on three bones that I had given him the other day, ones discarded in the River Acheron. Father bent down and patted Cerberus on one of his heads. "You did good today. You deserve something a little special."

With a snap of his fingers, a large bone appeared in front of the puppy. All of his eyes widened, and each head howled a thank you before biting down on the new bone. I tried not to appear frustrated as it had taken me weeks to find the bone I had already given him. But it didn't matter, Cerberus looked so happy as all three of his heads tried to snap at each other, wanting the bone to itself.

I stepped outside with my father, looking upon all the Underworld from the patio. The dark sparkling water of Oceanus made up all the sky, and beyond that laid the human world, Earth. I had never seen yet, but one day wanted to. It was where all the deceased came from, a place that I only learned about in books and from tutors. Coming down in the middle of the clouds was the waterfall of Phlegethon, souls in a blue fire all destined for Tartarus, the enormous gaping hole that didn't seem to ever have an end. They were all the wicked souls, the souls that had no chance at redemption. If I listened closely, I could hear their cries for help. Then again, that could have been the River Cocytus. It sounded like the wind, or at least that was what Huntley said, I wouldn't know.

Next, around River Phlegethon, was the palace itself. This was where I lived and spent most of my time. Since we had visitors every once in a while, Father was hesitant to even let me venture outside the palace. The palace was big, of course, as it held many of those who were more like guests than the deceased, although some weren't dead, like Hermes for example. How he got into the Underworld, Father could never figure out. It pissed him off every time Hermes showed up with a smirk on his face. Many beings were sent to search for the loophole that Hermes had found, but none figured it out. I always had to be cautious, though, as Hermes couldn't know I existed, especially since he was a kiss-up to Zeus, at least according to Father.

A lot of the others had been my tutors over the years, ranging from teaching me languages, history, culture, math, etc. I never understood why I needed to know these things, specifically since I never got to leave this realm.

The palace itself looked like something out of *Van Helsing*. One of my tutors called it 'a late gothic German style architecture like that of Eltz Castle'. Huntley said, 'holy fuck, it's Dracula's castle!'. I liked his description better. Also, calling it Dracula's castle made it easier to spook him with.

I loved it here and I could even watch some human movies in the Underworld. It was confusing though, as none were consistent with each other. I never could tell fact from fiction either, especially since those on Earth say the Underworld is a fictitious place. I loved seeing their faces when they found out the truth.

Beyond my home were the Elysian Fields and the

Asphodel Meadows, where the good souls along with okay souls went. The Elysian Fields were nice, but I preferred the palace. And I wouldn't know what Tartarus was like because no one ever came back from there, at least not very often.

I stepped up to the railing next to Father. He wore his normal all-black suit and tie. Don't get me wrong, he looked good in black, but sometimes I just wished for a little more color. I was wearing an all-black dress, so I couldn't really talk. Then again, I only wore it because he insisted on it during the judging.

Also, my father wasn't bad looking. He had a chiseled jaw, high cheekbones, and good teeth. I mean, I wouldn't really know if he was good or bad looking, but that was what the maids said. Many of them didn't think my mother deserved such a beautiful god, as she was gone from this place nine months of the year, not to mention she snuck countless men in here during the three months she was here. Most of the workers called her a whore, and I didn't bother to blame or correct them.

"Why do you even have those sessions?" I decided I would be the first to talk. I hated it when we just stood there in silence. "You always sentence them to Tartarus."

He smiled, as if my question was comical. He wasn't as bad as people made him out to be. He was quite kind actually, and it wasn't his fault that Zeus sentenced him to rule over this part of the world. Although, when given the circumstances, he could turn dark in just a blink of an eye and show absolutely no mercy.

Which was why I never got on his bad side. At least, not completely.

"You know it's not that simple, my precious flower. There are some that are judged that do, in fact, deserve some sort of paradise instead of eternal torment. I can't let them get wrongly judged. You understand that, don't you?"

I let out a brief sigh. I understood, as we had gone over this many times before. I just hated sitting there, watching those stooges be idiots. I wondered whether I could pick new judges when Father passed on his legacy to me. Probably not since Zeus appointed them himself, and they were Zeus' sons, as were a good chunk of souls down here, and if I fired them, then Zeus would find out and I would be screwed.

Because I was never supposed to be born.

"I know," I mumbled.

He wrapped his arm around my shoulder and kissed my forehead. "Your mother will be coming home tonight. Are you excited?"

I tried not to roll my eyes, I truly did, but yeah, I rolled my eyes. Hard. Yes, I loved my mother, for the most part, and yes, I knew she cared for me in her own little way. But after having to deal with her drama for hundreds of years, I was getting sick of her.

Hades seemed disappointed with my lack of enthusiasm. "What's that look for? Don't you miss her?"

I looked up at the souls that came raining down into the Underworld and toward their destination through the River Acheron. "It's just hard to miss someone who, while here, only talks about Earth, all the things she sees and buys. She'd rather be part of that world than this one, even when the two of us are here. It doesn't make me feel like she wants to be with me."

"Your mother cares a lot about you, she's just bad at expressing it."

"And what about you? Do you really think she cares about you?" It was a harsh thing of me to ask, but it was also harsh of him to give her the benefit of the doubt.

"She does… in her own way."

I couldn't believe he was defending her after all these years. "She leaves for nine months of the year, Father. *Nine months.* In those nine months, you know she's sleeping with other men. Along with that, while she is here, she *sneaks* men in and has affairs with them. You know how many men of hers I have run into over the years? She doesn't want to be here anymore than I do—" I covered my mouth. I didn't mean to say that, it just slipped out.

Hades looked at me, his eyes alert, waiting to see if I would say anything else. His body seemed tight, reacting to the words I had let out by accident. "You… you don't like it here either?"

"No, I do. This is your world, Father, everything you have built. I would want nothing else. Except…" I began, trying to find the right words. "I would like to see the Earth, or Olympus. I want to know what else is out there. I just learn about them from tutors, but I would like to experience it for myself. See the ocean, the sky… It's my dream."

He studied me closely. "You know that isn't possible, you know if you leave this place you will no longer be under my protection. The gods could hurt you, they will find out you exist and they will take you away from me."

I gave him one of my 'don't worry, I won't do

anything stupid' smiles. "I know. I didn't say I would leave. I'm just saying that hopefully someday I can."

"So you won't leave me like everyone else?" For the first time, I saw the sadness in his eyes, the loneliness that came with his title being brought to the surface. It was why he didn't care what Persephone did behind his back, why he was willing to put up with it for the short time they had together during the year.

Why he cared for me so much and why he hid me from the other gods.

"No, never. I love you Father, nothing will ever change that."

He wrapped his arms around me. "The other reason I could never be mad at your mother is because she gave me the best thing I could ever ask for. My little flower in this dark world." He stepped back and smiled as he moved a piece of hair out of my face. "Now you better get going or you will be late for your tutoring lesson."

I smiled and nodded, hurrying off before he questioned what we would be tutoring, making me lie yet again. He couldn't, no he would never know, that Huntley and I would be playing some soccer instead of learning current earthly events.

But soccer was current, right? Yeah, I would keep telling myself that, otherwise I fear I would lose my mind being stuck here.

Thank you for reading! Be sure to check it out at your local or online retailer!

Acknowledgements

I am so excited to finally finish this series! I started it with my friend Corinne in middle school in 2004ish, so it definitely has been in the making for a long while. It was a bunch of middle school garbage and full of my favorite actors and places I wanted to go. I was obsessed with *Star Wars* at the time, and still am, so I loved science fiction. I am thankful for my friends who read my book, gave me feed back, and told me I would never finish it. That made me want to prove them wrong and I never stopped writing.

I also want to say thank you everyone in my writing group along with all my writing mentors through the few years I have been taking classes and joining programs. They have taught me a lot and helped me keep on going. I love having them to talk to, cry to, and cuss to.

A big thank you to my editor Justin and my cover artist from Biserka Designs. With both your help, this series was made possible!

Thank you to my friends Faye and V who helped me get this series actually published and helped with beta reading and promoting my books. I couldn't have done it without you.

Lastly, thank you to my parents and my husband. Without your support this wouldn't have been possible.

About the Author

Dani Hoots is a science fiction, fantasy, romance, and young adult author who loves anything with a story. She has a B.S. in Anthropology, a Masters of Urban and Environmental Planning, a Certificate in Novel Writing from Arizona State University, and a BS in Herbal Science from Bastyr University.

Currently she is working on a YA urban fantasy series called Daughter of Hades, a YA urban fantasy series called The Wonderland Chronicles, a historic fantasy vampire series called A World of Vampires, and a YA sci-fi series called Sanshlian Series. She has also started up an indie publishing company called FoxTales Press. She also works with Anthill Studios in creating comics through Antik Comics.

Her hobbies include reading, watching anime, cooking, studying different languages, wire walking, hula hoop, and working with plants. She is also an herbalist and sells her concoctions on FoxCraft Apothecary. She lives in Phoenix with her husband and visits Seattle often.

Feel free to email her with any questions you might have!
danihootsauthor@gmail.com